TEXAS LEGENDS ★ BOOK 2

ALSO BY GENE SHELTON

Texas Legends: Book One *Last Gun*

Captain Jack

The Story
of John Coffee Hays

GENE SHELTON

A DOUBLE D WESTERN
DOUBLEDAY
New York London Toronto Sydney Auckland

A Double D Western

PUBLISHED BY DOUBLEDAY

a division of Bantam Doubleday Dell Publishing Group, Inc.
666 Fifth Avenue, New York, New York 10103

Double D Western, Doubleday,
and the portrayal of the letters DD
are trademarks of Doubleday, a division of
Bantam Doubleday Dell Publishing Group, Inc.

Library of Congress Cataloging-in-Publication Data

Shelton, Gene.
    Captain Jack: the story of John Coffee Hays/by Gene Shelton.
    1st ed.
        p.   cm.—(Texas legends; bk. 2)   (A Double D western)
    1. Hays, John Coffee, 1817–1883—Fiction. 2. Texas Rangers—History—
Fiction. 3. Texas—History—1846–1950—Fiction. I. Series.
PS3569.H39364C36   1991
813′.54—dc20   91-3743
CIP

ISBN 0-385-41411-0

10 9 8 7 6 5 4 3 2 1

To my wife, Barbara—

With thanks for her tolerance, encouragement and affection during all these years together, this work is dedicated in love and respect.

—GENE SHELTON

FOREWORD

This is a work of fiction based on the life of Captain John Coffee Hays, the man who set the standard by which Texas Rangers have been judged since the 1830s.

Many of the individuals portrayed in this work actually existed, but the reader should draw no conclusions as to their actual characters, motivations and actions on the basis of this story.

Numerous other characters and events herein are purely the creation of the author.

Every effort has been made, within the framework of the fiction novel, to portray as accurately as possible the actual dates, locations and sequence of events that shaped the life of Jack Hays and his role in the history of the state of Texas.

ACKNOWLEDGMENTS

The author wishes to express his appreciation to the many librarians, fellow members of the Western Writers of America, Inc., other historians whose assistance and scholarly works made this book possible and the staff of the Moody Texas Ranger Library in Waco, Texas.

Readers who wish to pursue in greater detail the life and times of John Coffee Hays and the early Texas Rangers are urged to consult Webb's *The Texas Rangers;* Fehrenbach's *Lone Star: A History of Texas and the Texans;* Singletary's *The Mexican War;* Bauer's *Zachary Taylor;* and Wilson's *C-O-L-T: An American Legend.* While these eminent historians may not agree on all details, their works were invaluable to the author in the preparation of this story.

CAPTAIN JACK

ONE

North Llano River
Republic of Texas
July 1839

The westerly breeze spilled down from the Sacramento mountains, magnified the heat waves that swirled past the cross hairs of the field transit and blurred the edges of the red and white target disk on the pole in the rodman's hand.

Jack Hays squinted through the optics and made the notation in his field survey book: twenty chains, twelve links. Just over thirteen hundred twenty feet, about as far as a surveyor could push his instruments and his own talent under such conditions, he conceded.

He closed the leather-bound field book and waved a signal for the chainman to stake the spot. He reached for the level knob, the first step in breaking down the transit to move to a new base —and paused as a barely distinct smear on the foothills to the west caught his attention. He swung the instrument toward the blur and peered through the tube.

The blur came into focus, fragmented by wind and heat waves, but distinct enough in the frontiersman's eye.

"What is it, Mister Hays?"

Jack Hays glanced at the thin, sunburned face of the man at his side. Jules Delorette was new to the frontier if not to the surveying trade, a nervous man who saw rattlesnakes in every bush and tarantulas behind every rock. There was no doubt about the man's ability; he had been schooled at William & Mary, his mathematics were impeccable and his survey methods precise. But more than that was needed on the frontier.

Jack had battled misgivings about the Canadian-born Frenchman from the first day out of San Antonio, but a man didn't refuse a personal request from President Lamar.

"Smoke. About two miles northwest in the foothills."

"Smoke? A prairie fire, perhaps?"

"Not likely." Jack twirled the level knob, loosened the thumb screws and lifted the transit unit from the swivel plate. "Too small for a grass fire. My guess would be Comanches."

Delorette's face blanched beneath the sunburn. "Wild Indians? My God—what do we do now?"

Jack finished breaking down the transit, stored it with care in the sturdy wood and leather case at his feet, then waved toward the crew members in the distance, beckoning them to him. He turned again to the Frenchman.

"We go take a look, Mister Delorette," Jack said, his voice calm and matter-of-fact. "One of the rules of the Texas frontier. Someone could be in trouble over there." Jack strode to the waiting horses and slipped the transit case into the special carry rig on the sorrel packhorse.

"But, Mister Hays, there are only eight of us. There could be a hundred Indians out there!"

Jack tugged the final strap tight on the pack animal. "Not likely. Raiding party, maybe, or hunters. Besides, we don't know for sure it's Comanches. If it is, eight of us should be enough."

Delorette's protest drowned beneath the thud of horse's hooves on the short-grass prairie. William Alexander Anderson Wallace, the surveying party's chief scout and hunter, reined his big rawboned bay to a sliding stop six feet from Jack Hays.

"You see it, Jack?" Bigfoot Wallace's normally jovial face was set in a scowl. There was no hint of the laughter that usually lay just beneath the Virginia drawl. Bigfoot Wallace took his Indians seriously.

"I saw it," Jack said. He looked up at the scout. Considerably up. Bigfoot Wallace stood six feet two and weighed two-forty, all of it muscle and bone, in sharp contrast to Jack's lean five-nine frame that carried barely a hundred and sixty pounds. The difference in size did not diminish the mutual respect between the big frontiersman and the Tennessee-born surveyor. "What do you make of it, Bigfoot?"

Wallace's thick eyebrows bunched as he stared toward the northwest. "Smoke in Comanche country don't mean but one thing. Trouble. You call the others in?"

Jack nodded, walked to his own horse and lifted a big single-shot pistol from its saddle holster. He checked the load and cap, repeated the procedure with a second pistol, then with the fifty-eight-caliber rifle. Satisfied, he returned the weapons to their scabbards. The pistols hung on each side of the saddle pommel. The rifle nested in a rawhide case by his right stirrup.

All members of the survey party were armed, but none more than Bigfoot Wallace. He carried a big-bore Pennsylvania rifle, a pair of horse pistols on each side of his saddle, a smaller handgun in his belt and a heavy, thick-bladed knife of the style developed by Jim Bowie. The packhorses carried a half-dozen spare pistols, two extra rifles, powder, ball and percussion caps along with the axes, shovels, picks and other tools of the surveyor's trade.

Jules Delorette's weapons were as out of place on the frontier as the man. He carried a fine English fowling piece with floral engraving and a pair of small-caliber French dueling pistols in a fancy rosewood case. The case already showed the scratches and gouges of field work. Delorette's fingers trembled as he reached for his powder horn and cap box. Jules dropped the ramrod twice before the weapons were finally loaded. Jack bit back the urge to chastise Delorette for carrying an unloaded gun in the first place. Jack hadn't thought it would be necessary to tell anyone that an unloaded gun was nothing more than a club.

Jack glanced at Bigfoot Wallace. The scout raised his gaze toward the sky in mock prayer and shook his head in disgust. The trio waited in silence as the remainder of the survey party regrouped around Jack. Five minutes later, the column of eight men rode at a slow trot toward the distant smoke.

• • • •

Jack Hays swallowed against the bitter taste in the back of his throat. The sound of Jules Delorette vomiting his guts out behind him didn't help.

The ruins of the small cabin smouldered in a sun-baked flat below scrub-covered foothills. The woman's body lay just outside the door. She had been raped and mutilated, her breasts cut off and abdomen sliced open. An older man lay spread-eagled on the bare ground a few feet away. Small embers piled atop his groin still trickled smoke. The skin had been stripped from his armpits to his waist. Flies buzzed about the raw sockets where his eyes had been. A boy barely in his teens had been spared the long agony of the adults; his head was split like a dropped melon, shattered by a war axe. The blow must have killed him instantly. It also spoiled an overeager brave's trophy. The boy's scalp had been all but destroyed.

A sheep bleated forlornly in the distance. The Mexican family's small flock was scattered, many of them dead from lance or arrow. Killed for sport. There were no Sheep-Eater Indians in this part of the West.

Jack Hays, kneeling at the dead man's side, glanced up as Bigfoot Wallace rode in, his scout completed.

"Comanche, all right," Wallace said. "Paneteka band."

Jack stood and wiped a trace of blood from his fingers. "How many and how long ago?"

"I read fourteen. Six, maybe seven hours back, headed toward the Sacramentos." Wallace rolled a cud of tobacco to the other side of his jaw and spat. "They got a captive. Girl maybe twelve, thirteen years old, if I ain't forgot how to read sign."

Jack wiped the sweat from his forehead, removed his hat and ran his fingers through his thick black hair. "Can we catch up to them, Bigfoot?"

"Yep. They don't seem to be in no hurry. Kind of satisfied with themselves, I reckon. We can make 'em by sunup tomorrow. If they act like normal Comanch, that is."

Ralph Winzen, the broad-shouldered chainman, grunted in disgust. "Why bother? This is just a bunch of Mexicans. Good riddance in my book."

Jack spun on a heel to face Winzen, a sharp retort on his

tongue. Bigfoot Wallace beat him to it. "Dammit, Winzen," Wallace snapped, "there ain't a man alive hates Mexicans worse than me. I lost a brother and a cousin to the butchers at Goliad, and I come out here to even the score. But that young girl they got wasn't at Goliad. She wasn't at the Alamo. And, by God, I ain't gonna set here and let no damn Comanch abuse no child, white or brown!"

The chainman flushed and dropped his gaze under the cold glare of Wallace's slate-colored eyes.

"Bigfoot's right, Winzen," Jack said. "You know how the Comanches, and the Paneteka in particular, treat young women. Twelve, thirteen is just prime with them where captive girls are concerned." Jack paused to shake away the image that tried to form in his mind. *Maybe if we get there soon enough she won't suffer too much, one way or the other,* he thought. He stared toward the rocky, juniper-studded mountains. "If we don't stop this bunch, they may wind up with Texan scalps. Rattlers aren't particular who they bite."

Jules Delorette sagged against his horse, holding an arm across his aching belly. "My God! How can one human being do this to another?"

Wallace shrugged and spat. "No white man around these parts ever called any Comanche a human being, far as I know." The big scout turned to Jack. "Can't be sure, Jack," he said, "but I think this may be Half Hand's bunch."

Jack bit back a curse. Half Hand had lost a couple of fingers to a farm woman's axe three years ago. The mutilation at the hands of a mere woman had done something to the Paneteka sub-chief's mind. In all the Texas frontier there was no one Indian more hated or feared. His revenge against the whites—and women in particular—had been bitter. And ugly.

"Jack, we may not get another crack at that red bastard." Jack heard his own quiet rage reflected in Bigfoot Wallace's tone.

Jack toed the stirrup and mounted his Tennessee-bred sorrel. The horse snorted and shied, wide-eyed, but behaved himself at a sharp word from the rider. The gelding had been bred for speed and staying power, the kind of horse a man needed when his life depended on the animal between his knees. Still, he "had spirit," which was the Texas way of saying he'd buck your butt off if you didn't keep your bluff in on him. That was one reason he'd earned the name Judas.

"Anybody here doesn't want a piece of Half Hand," Jack said, "it's not but a hundred-twenty miles or so back to San Antonio. Bigfoot and I are going hunting."

No one in the group objected. They were frontier veterans, except for Jules Delorette, and the Frenchman obviously had no inclination to travel alone in Indian country. Jack could read the Texans' deadly mood in the set of jaw, the dark stares toward the nearby mountains.

Jack touched a knee to the leggy sorrel. "We'll bury these folks on the way back. Let's just hope the girl's still alive when we get there. And after we leave."

Jack Hays studied the Indian camp below in the gray pre-dawn light. The fourteen Comanche warriors were still asleep, wrapped in blankets against the chill morning air. No man was at his best—even an Indian—when jarred from slumber by an unexpected attack. Groggy minds and full bladders took the edge off men coming out of a deep sleep.

In the center of the camp the young girl huddled without blankets, tethered by horsehair ropes to a stake. A Comanche slept near her feet. Jack could only hope the Indians had not already slashed the tendons above the girl's heels to keep her from trying to run. If they had, she would be a cripple for life, even if they were able to get her out alive.

Jack was satisfied with his plan. The Comanches were accustomed to fighting the white man on a predictable basis. The Texans routinely rode into sight of the Indians, spurred horses within rifle range, dismounted, fired, reloaded, remounted and charged again. This time the Indians would fight on different terms. Jack Hays's terms.

He and four others had ridden the night out to reach the west side of the Comanche camp undetected. They would hit the Indian camp fighting solely from horseback. With luck, they could grab the captive before the Comanches had time to kill her, then make a run for the narrow canyon to the east of the Indian encampment.

In the rocky, cedar-covered canyon, two of the best marksmen in Jack's survey party waited, each with a spare rifle from the packs. Jack, the girl and his handful of men were the bait. The rifles in the canyon were the trap.

Each of the four men with Jack carried two of the big single-shot horse pistols. Their rifles would stay sheathed during the charge. This would be close work. Handgun and knife work.

Jules Delorette's job was to hold the pack mounts. Jack couldn't shake his doubts about Jules. He didn't know if the Frenchman could handle the tension alone and control the horses, or if he would panic and turn the whole thing sour. *Too late to worry about it now,* he told himself. He glanced at the men squatting beside him. Winzen's broad face was creased in a deep frown as he stared toward the Indian camp. Baker, the rodman, and Turner, a Methodist lay minister who had no equal with a pistol, waited in silence. Winzen and Baker would stampede the Comanche horses while Turner, Wallace and Jack charged straight into the middle of the Indian camp.

Wallace's big body seemed relaxed, his deep gray eyes calm but alert. Jack wondered if the frontiersman was caught up in the same curious, detached ease he himself felt before a fight. It was a strange sensation. The muscles were loose, the mind alert, senses sharp; the scratchy scurry of a beetle on a rock at Jack's elbow seemed loud to his ears. He wondered idly if this was the way a cougar felt in the final, careful steps of the stalk.

"Bigfoot," Jack said softly, "I'll try for the girl first. You back me up. Sometimes Judas gets a little crazy when a gun goes off in his ear."

"Okay, Jack. One of these days you're going to have to get yourself a good war pony or you'll get a lance up your butt." Wallace chuckled softly. "Reckon it's time to wake up some Comanches?"

Jack nodded. "No reason a man should sleep all day. Let's mount up."

The five men held their horses to a slow, steady walk as they approached the camp. Winzen and Baker reined their mounts toward the Comanche pony herd. The Texans were within thirty yards of the sleeping Indians before one of the braves stirred, looked up and yelped.

Jack drove his spurs into the gelding. Judas stumbled, then

broke into a hard run, ears pinned back along his neck. At his side, Jack heard Bigfoot Wallace sound the Texan war whoop. The Indian guarding the girl scrambled from his blanket and reached for a bow. Jack fired at the Indian's chest. The heavy ball slammed the Comanche to the ground. Jack jammed the pistol under his belt, whipped his knife from its sheath and pulled hard on the reins. For once, Judas behaved himself. The horse slid to a stop beside the stake. Jack leaned from the saddle, whipped the blade through the horsehair rope which bound the girl, grabbed her by an arm and yanked her roughly across Judas's withers, face-down in front of the saddle. An arrow buzzed past Jack's ear. He leaned forward and touched spurs to Judas.

Jack had no time to sort out the flow of battle. He heard the flat crack of pistol shots, Wallace's and Turner's whoops, Winzen's shouts and the thud of hooves as the Comanche ponies broke the tether line and bolted. Then Jack and the captive girl were past the edge of the Indian camp. A second arrow whirred past Jack's shoulder. He glanced back to see Wallace's horse run down and trample one brave; steel flashed as the frontiersman leaned from the saddle, his Bowie knife ripping open a second Indian's belly.

Two hundred yards into the canyon, Jack eased his horse to a stop and lifted the girl from Judas's withers. The brown eyes that stared back at him were wide in terror. Raw burn marks marred the tender young skin of small breasts exposed by the torn cloth of her coarse dress. Jack didn't want to know what other horrors the child had endured in the past few hours. He noted in relief that she hadn't been hamstrung; her thighs were bloody but her legs were intact.

"It is all right, little one," Jack said in Spanish. "You are with friends. We will take you to a safe place. No one will hurt you now."

Tears welled in the girl's eyes as the wall of pain and shock slowly crumbled. She put her arms around Jack's neck and squeezed as though he might slip from her grasp. He felt her shoulders jerk in a sob against his chest. He stroked the tangled brown hair as he kneed Judas into a lope. *At least, by God, they've paid a price for what they did to her,* he thought, *and they'll pay more before the morning is out.* He glanced over his shoulder at the sound of horses approaching on the run. Bigfoot Wallace and Turner had fought clear of the camp, the other two men close behind. The side of Turner's head was awash in blood.

"Turner, are you all right?"

The lay minister swabbed blood from the corner of his eye with a sleeve and loosed a string of curses that would bring envy from a bull-whacker. Jack knew then the man wasn't seriously hurt. "Let the horses blow a minute or two," Jack said, "then we'll finish this dance. Anybody see Half Hand?"

His question brought head shakes and negative grunts all around. Jack cursed silently as he set a deliberate pace up the canyon. Distant shouts and cries from the Comanche camp changed timbre from surprise and pain to anger as the pursuit organized. Winzen and Baker had spooked most of the ponies, but some had been hobbled or securely staked away from the horsehair rope picket line. Others wouldn't stray far. And there were some thoroughly mad Comanches back there.

A half-dozen mounted Indians were on the chase within minutes. The Texans kept a measured lead a hundred yards out of bow range and reloaded their weapons as they rode.

"There's Half Hand," Bigfoot said after a glance back at the pursuit. "The ugly sonofabitch on the gray horse."

The Comanches rode straight into the trap. Rifles cracked from the canyon walls. One Indian tumbled from his horse, another went down with his mount as a heavy ball tore into the animal's chest. Wallace spurred ahead, slipped his long gun from its sheath, dismounted and knelt. Smoke belched from the rifle. Half Hand twisted, almost fell from his horse, then righted himself and whipped the gray toward the cover of a thicket along a canyon wall. Jack heard Wallace's sharp oath. Bigfoot seldom missed a dead-center hit at that range, even at a running target. The remaining Indians spun their horses about and raced back toward the mouth of the canyon, the chase abandoned.

Jack snorted the smell of powder smoke and dust from his nostrils. Half Hand's band had been bloodied. The fight was gone from them now. Comanches might be the deadliest fighters of the Plains tribes, but they weren't stupid. None of them were in a big hurry to die, and they didn't like a fight when the odds weren't heavily in their favor. Especially when their medicine had gone this bad.

Jack breathed a sigh of relief as he neared the top of the canyon trail—then yelped and yanked Judas hard left as a cloud of bird shot ripped past his head.

"Dammit, Jules! Put that scattergun down, you idiot!"

Delorette's pale face blanched even more. "I—I'm sorry—I didn't know—"

Jack reined the sorrel alongside Jules and glared in cold anger at the Frenchman. "Out here, Delorette, you know what you're shooting at before you pull the trigger." Jack choked back the urge to pistol-whip the man. "I didn't ride through a dozen Comanches just to get shot by some wet-eared greenhorn."

"I'm so terribly sorry, Mister Hays—"

"Shut up, Jules. Just shut up. Now."

Jack let the surge of anger drain from his body. The danger was over. Staying mad wasn't going to solve a thing. Anger clouded a man's judgment.

Jules Delorette slumped with head down, cowed.

A few minutes later Jack Hays stood before his men, the Mexican girl clinging to his waist. He was satisfied. His best guess was five Comanches dead, Half Hand and a couple of others wounded.

"Will they come after us, Jack?" Winzen asked.

"I doubt it. We kicked the fight out of them for now, at least."

Jack's own party was in surprisingly good shape, considering the circumstances. A glancing blow of a war axe had ripped the skin above Turner's ear. The blood flow made the cut seem worse than it was. Winzen cleaned the gash with a cloth from the pack and tied a bandage into place. Turner had a ringing headache but his eyes were clear. The rodman would be all right. No one else had been so much as scratched, and only one horse hurt—an arrow wound in a shoulder. Bigfoot Wallace tended the horse. Jack knew the animal was in good hands.

"Gentlemen," Jack said, "you did well today. That's one raiding party that won't bedevil the frontier for some time. Half Hand escaped, but he's lost face. It'll be a long time before any braves will trust him to lead a raid again." He pried the girl's arms free of his waist, lifted her onto one of the spare horses and

mounted. "Let's get on our way. We've some people to bury."
He turned to Wallace. "Bigfoot, I'd like you to keep an eye on
the girl. Keep her away while we bury her folks. I don't want her
to have to go through more than she already has." He kneed
Judas back toward the burned shepherd's cabin.

The sun was near its midpoint when the final shovel of dirt fell
on the three graves. Turner, blood still seeping through the bandage around his skull, said a few words over the graves in both
Spanish and English, then recited in Latin as much of the Catholic funeral mass as he could remember. *It should be sufficient,* Jack
thought; *the Almighty will understand the lack of formality.*

Jules Delorette leaned against his shovel as sweat poured down
his thin face. His retching had finally stopped. Making Delorette
handle the bodies was Jack's way of punishing him for the indiscretion with the shotgun at the mouth of the canyon.

By noon the survey party had returned to the last stake driven
before the Indian troubles began. Jack retrieved his transit and
began to set up the instrument.

"Mister Hays," Turner said, "are we going to bobtail this survey?"

Jack half smiled at the question. On the frontier, bobtail
surveys weren't uncommon. The surveyor set one or two corners,
guessed at the remainder, and got the hell out of Indian country. "No, Turner. The Republic of Texas is paying for a full
survey, not a guess. But I want you and Bigfoot to take the girl
back to San Antonio. Turn her over to the priest. The church
will find her a safe home."

"Mister Hays, I—I could go back with Mister Wallace—"

Jack sighed as he glanced toward Jules Delorette. "No, Jules.
You signed on for this survey. You're going to finish it."

TWO

San Antonio
August 1839

Jack Hays factored in the correction for chain sag, referred to his field notes for the temperature reading on the final leg of the survey and calculated the chain stretch deviation for a ninety-two-degree day. He rechecked his computations and closed the survey with a pen stroke connecting the first and last observation points on the linen sheet tacked to his worktable. He sighed in satisfaction.

No survey was ever exact. That was accepted as a fact in his profession. There were always errors. Small errors in measurement, in pinpointing location by compass and sextant, the expansion of a chain by as much as a link on a hot day, the impossibility of stretching a chain perfectly level in defiance of gravity, all could compound into big mistakes in a hurry. But this survey was as close to perfection as could be expected. It closed to within five rods, an error of eighty-two and a half feet over a linear survey enclosing almost twelve thousand acres. The error was negligible. The Republic of Texas had gotten its money's worth.

He tilted his chair back, raised his gaze toward the ceiling and flexed his shoulders to ease the slight ache between his shoulder blades. The math part of surveying wasn't nearly as much fun as the field work, he thought. It chained a man to a desk, and a hard wooden chair didn't have the lively feel of a good horse between the knees. Judas could be a pain in the butt, but he *was* a good horse. Most of the time.

He glanced up at a knock on the door frame of the two-room stone shack which doubled as his office and home. The wooden door was open against the heat of the afternoon. The stocky frame of Colonel Henry W. Karnes, Texas Mounted Rifles, blocked most of the light from the door. Sunlight cast a halo around the shock of unkempt red hair that a number of Comanches coveted as a scalp lock. None had lived to get close enough to collect it.

"Come in, Colonel." Jack rose from his chair and extended a hand. Karnes's calloused grip was firm almost to the point of being painful; the commanding officer of the San Antonio volunteer company didn't realize how physically strong he was. The officer's face showed the pink tinge of perpetual sunburn that plagued those of fair skin, no matter how much time they spent in sun and wind. The tint seemed to emphasize the depth of Karnes's gold-flecked green eyes.

Jack motioned to a chair. "Have a seat, Colonel Karnes. I'd offer you something to drink, but I don't keep any liquor around and I just finished the last of the coffee."

Karnes waved a hand. "No matter, Jack." The colonel eased himself into a chair and stroked his heavy chin. "This is sort of a business call."

"Survey work?"

Karnes shook his head. "I'm afraid it's nothing that lucrative. I've gone over your report on the fight with Half Hand. Interesting tactics you came up with."

Jack shrugged. "It was the only way I could see to get the girl out alive."

"That you did. I don't think anyone else, myself included, could have managed it." The colonel leaned back in his chair. "I'll come right to the point. I could use a man like you in the volunteer rifles, Jack. You're bright, young—what is it, twenty-three?"

Jack nodded. "Close enough. Will be in January."

"I need men who can think on the run, react to situations as they develop. Men who know horses and how to use terrain and weapons to advantage. And," Karnes concluded, "men who are single. A man worried about a wife or a sick child isn't at his best in the field."

Jack smiled. "Well, Colonel, you may have me overrated in a lot of categories, but at least I don't have a wife."

"That will likely change one day, if an Indian or a Mexican doesn't kill you in the meantime." Karnes sighed. The green eyes seemed to hold an apology. "I'm asking a lot of you, to give up a good surveying practice for the pleasure of being shot at, sleeping in the mud and snow, supplying your own horse and weapons, spending twelve to twenty hours a day in the saddle, and eating ground corn, dried beef and dust. That's on the better days. They're usually worse. In addition to letting you enjoy these many pleasures, the Republic will pay you the magnificent sum of a dollar and a quarter a day. Provided Texas has the money to pay, that is."

Jack smiled. "I'm flattered that you asked, but—"

Karnes lifted a hand. "Hear me out, Jack. I'm not asking for an answer today. I'm not much of a recruiter, but I think you understand that the Republic of Texas has more troubles than a man carrying a live bobcat by a hind leg."

Karnes stood and walked to the map tacked behind Jack's desk. "We've got Mexicans to the south wanting their country back." He stabbed a blunt finger south of the Nueces River, the border between Mexico and Texas. "It's not a question of *if* they come. It's a question of *when* they come." The finger drifted up the Nueces past the Balcones Escarpment into the Hill Country north and west of San Antonio. "We've got Indians from here clear onto the *Llano Estacado,* the Staked Plains. Hardly a day passes the Comanches don't raid a Texas family somewhere."

The colonel fell silent for a moment, studying the map, then turned to Jack. "Texas can't afford to put a regular army in the field, Jack. The Republic is broke. That means it's up to us, the volunteers—the ranging companies—to protect our people until the United States comes to its senses and annexes Texas." Karnes's frown deepened. "It may be quite a while before that happens. And we're the only line of defense until the politicians get off their butts and do something." The colonel snorted in disgust. "Hell, our own politicians can't decide where they stand or what to do."

Karnes plucked his hat from the peg by the door. "That's about as simple as it gets, Jack. The future of Texas is up to Texans. That's why we need men like you in the ranging companies. Will you think it over?"

"Of course I will, Colonel," Jack said. "I'll let you know as soon as I get back from filing the Beale survey with the land office in Houston—if that's where the capital is this week. It gets moved more often than a monte dealer's bottom card."

Karnes winced. "With all our other problems, you'd think our duly elected leaders would have something better to do than argue about where the seat of government belongs. Half of 'em want Austin for the capital, the other half want Houston. Personally, I don't give a damn as long as we get a place to call home. It's like watching two kids fight over the last hard candy in the dish." Karnes clamped his hat on his head, then glanced around. "Where's your associate? Mister Delorette?"

"We had a little talk last week, Colonel. We decided he would be more comfortable practicing his trade back east. Where the chances of getting snakebit, scalped, shot, skinned or lanced aren't quite so high. He's an excellent surveyor but not cut from frontier cloth. I wish him well."

The colonel grunted an agreement, started toward the door, then paused. "May I ask you a personal question, Jack?"

"Of course."

"Why did you come to Texas? A man with your education and training could find work anywhere in the civilized world."

Jack Hays smiled and shrugged. "Anywhere isn't always the best place to be, Colonel Karnes. I like it here. It isn't so crowded a man can't breathe. And I haven't been bored on the Texas frontier."

Karnes accepted the explanation at face value. Jack watched the ranging company leader leave and pondered his parting question. He didn't consider himself an adventurer, but there had always been the call of the frontier in his soul, the lure of not knowing what was beyond the next river or hill and having a chance to find out. On the fringe of civilization, a man was what he was, good or bad, and was accepted—or hanged—for it. No excuses were necessary. Out here a man was expected to tell the truth, even if the truth had a few warts on it. It wasn't necessary to play politics on the frontier, to tell some man in power what he wanted to hear instead of where the skunk really slept.

Jack wandered back to his desk, plucked a pen staff from the clutter and turned the writing instrument in his fingers. Texas had a powerful appeal to all kinds of men. Men like Bowie, Travis, Crockett and the hundred-eighty-five others who had spat their contempt at death from an old mission only a short walk from this office. Men like Ben Milam, who had died in the early days of the Battle of San Antonio, shot through the head in the doorway of the Viramendi Palace nearby. And a few men who were only a step ahead of the law when they crossed the Sabine River, looking for a new life. Or fresh victims.

There were a surprising number of professional men as well. Doctors, lawyers, merchants, educators. A whole range of "civilized" men, all with the same itch Jack Hays had needed to scratch. Here a man could debate the qualities of a horse or a gun or the philosophy of Plato or Virgil, or Shakespeare's observations on human nature, often with the same companion and without rancor.

Texas had the coldest winters, hottest summers, bitingest bugs, thorniest branches, richest croplands, best grass, finest orchards. Good water, bad water, and in many places no water at all. Game animals by the thousands, rivers rich with fish. A man could find a spot which suited him whether he preferred coastal swamp, arid desert or mountains. *It's Texas,* Jack Hays thought, *and nothing more need be said.*

He sighed, signed the final survey plat and gently blotted the ink dry. He rolled the document with care and tied it with a scrap of white ribbon.

Colonel Karnes had been right in more ways than one, Jack mused. Texas was at war on three fronts. To the south, Mexico still smarted from Sam Houston's defeat of Santa Anna and the subsequent loss of Texas. An invasion force could come at any moment across the Nueces River. Some Texans, still feeling the flush of victory at San Jacinto, discounted the Mexican Army as a worthy adversary.

Jack Hays knew different.

The Mexican regulars were career soldiers, skilled in the arts of war, well drilled and dedicated. Their mounted troops were the equal of the Southern Comanche as horsemen. Only the massive ego of their general had cost them Texas. Any military leader except Santa Anna would have simply bypassed the Alamo, left a token force to keep the volunteers trapped in the mission and moved on to eradicate the ill-equipped Texas army. Instead, Santa Anna had chosen to send wave after wave of assault troops against them. He had lost a third of his six-thousand-man army, and with them, the war. The Alamo had given Sam Houston thirteen days. Without those two weeks, Spanish would be the only language heard between the Sabine and the Pacific.

The butchery of the Texas captives at Goliad had been a serious mistake by the Mexicans. It had tempered the Texan's already sharp-edged hate and distrust of the Mexican. A man would fight harder for hate than for simple ideals. He would fight harder only to protect his own. Hate could be an edge. The atrocities of Mexican and Indian had put that edge on almost every Texan.

The Mexicans had to come back, Jack knew. The stakes were too high for them to ignore. Texas was the key to the West. If the Anglos kept Texas, the rest of Mexican claims from the Nueces to the Pacific Ocean were in jeopardy, and the Mexicans knew it. Only the internal squabbles for power in Mexico kept a massive invasion at bay for the moment. A united Mexico could swarm over the handful of whites in Texas in a matter of days under competent leadership.

On the northern and western frontiers of Texas the problem was red rather than brown. Comanche, Wichita, Kiowa, Pawnee, Apache and a half-dozen other Indian tribes boasted warriors trained from birth in the ways of battle. They tried—and sometimes succeeded—in pushing the white man from the hunting ranges and winter campgrounds. But the politics of the Indian was much like that of the Mexican. The tribes were too busy fighting each other to combine their forces and smash the whites.

Better make that four fronts, Jack thought. There were enemies back east as well, in the United States Congress. And even in Texas's own halls of state.

After independence, Texans had overwhelmingly approved a referendum seeking annexation to the United States. Action on that front was now stalled by several issues. The Republic's crushing debt was one. The slavery question was another. The free-staters in Congress opposed admission, even though Texas farmers and ranchers held less than three hundred Negro slaves.

Still, Texas had some leverage. The least logical to Jack was the view of some visionaries that Texas would become a global power, somehow manage to conquer the Southwest all the way through California. Reality aside, that prospect was feared in some business and political quarters on the East Coast. And Texas was gaining ground on the international scene. Britain and France liked the idea of a Texas Republic. Europe's insatiable demand for cotton could be supplied cheaper, and without excessive tariffs, from Texas than from the Union. Eventually, Jack knew, the United States would be forced to come around to annexation. Any other action would spit in the eye of logic.

Until then, it was a matter of survival. Jack could find no flaw in Karnes's reasoning. The future of a nation rested in the hands of a few volunteers. And now, Jack Hays had been invited to join an outmanned ranging company under circumstances any competent military tactician would regard as hopeless.

At the moment, too, the politics of the new Republic seemed to be sinking into a bottomless bog. The state was split in its political loyalties. The Peace Party's Sam Houston, who won his presidency and his fame in battle, feared standing armies and preached pacification of the Indians rather than extermination. Houston had the backing of the powerful East Texas planter faction. Mirabeau B. Lamar and his War Party favored a professional army, even though Texas could not afford one. His policy toward the Indian was the opposite of Houston's. No Indian, Lamar believed, could be pacified; they must be eliminated or pushed from Texas before peace could come to the state. Jack had to admit he leaned toward Lamar's Indian policy. Any man who trusted a Comanche was gambling his hair away.

Jack shook his attention back to the moment. He stowed the completed survey in a waterproof container for the trip to Houston and walked to the small window overlooking the main street of San Antonio.

There were few white faces in the traffic along the dusty thoroughfare lined with stone and adobe-stucco buildings.

Most of the pedestrians were Mexican laborers, shoulders slumped beneath heavy serapes and the floppy broad brims of high-crowned straw hats, heading home from the day's work in Anglo homes and gardens or the growing businesses that brought a measure of prosperity to the sleepy town that many still called Bexar. A few smiled at the whites. In others, suspicion or outright hate lay just below the surface of the dark eyes, as black as Jack's own. It was no wonder, Jack thought, that the whites of the town slept with pistol and knife at hand.

Mexicans were a strange breed where Texans were concerned. Most thought a Mexican could smile at you, call you friend, inquire of your family's health in a sincere tone and then slip a knife blade through your gizzard with no hesitation or remorse. Yet there had been Mexican Texans at the Alamo, and Mexican Texans had signed the Texas Declaration of Independence. Those men were considered heroes and compatriots among Anglos of the Republic. It was, Jack concluded, as though there were two separate races of Mexicans—"our Mexicans" and "their Mexicans."

Here and there along the street, a "tame" Indian lounged in the shade, Tonkawas, Lipans and Wacos for the most part, their lots now cast with the Texans against their traditional enemies of other tribes. Especially the Comanche. Nobody liked the Comanche. Except possibly the Kiowas, who were equally brutal and just as deadly.

Nearby a baby wailed for its mother. Jack idly wondered if the infant were one of those rare commodities, a native Texan with a white skin. It didn't matter, he thought. The child's cry was the song of the future. Texas would survive.

He leaned against the open window frame, smelled the dust of the street, the scent of horse manure, the spicy aroma of Mexican cooking, the whiff of fresh-baked bread that set the mouth to watering, all played against the distinctive tapestry of wood burning in fireplaces or in the open charcoal pits outside the bedraggled shacks of the poor. The smells of home, Jack thought, similar yet so unlike those in the rolling green hills of his youth in Little Cedar Lick, Tennessee, where he had been christened John Coffee Hays.

Jack turned away from the window, idly wondering how he could be so certain Texas would live. The odds weren't in its favor. It was just a feeling in the gut. Perhaps the passage from Voltaire expressed it best, he thought: "Faith consists in believing when it is beyond the power of reason to believe. It is not enough that a thing be possible for it to be believed."

Nueces River
September 1839

Texas Ranger Private John Coffee Hays squatted on his heels beside the small campfire in the pale light of dawn and waited for Colonel Henry Karnes to stamp into his boots. Jack glanced at the slab of venison on the green wood spit beside the fire. His stomach growled audibly. He hadn't eaten in more than twenty hours. He couldn't even remember the last time he'd slept.

"Any sign of Comanches, Jack?" Karnes jammed his short-crowned beaver hat onto his head to punctuate the question. Karnes looked as rumpled and dirty as the rest. In the field, a Ranger slept with his clothes on, his saddle and coat for a pillow, ammunition pouch and rifle at his side. Once the boots and hat were on, he was ready to ride or fight.

"Not an Indian in sight, Colonel," Jack said, rubbing a hand over the five-day growth of beard along his jaw. "But if you're interested in about seventy Mexican soldiers, I think I can be of service."

"Canales?"

Jack shook his head and saw the disappointment flash in Karnes's eyes. General Antonio Canales was rumored to be preparing another invasion of Texas. There wasn't a Texan drawing breath who didn't want a shot at the man known as the "Chaparral Fox," who had fouled the waters of many rivers with Anglo blood. "Didn't recognize the leader, but it wasn't Canales," Jack said. "Lancer detachment led by a captain." He reached for his knife and sliced off a palm-sized chunk of venison.

"Where?" Karnes pulled a battered map from his coat.

Jack touched the point of his knife to a spot on the rumpled linen south of the Nueces. "I first spotted their camp here." He moved the knife a few inches north to the junction of the Rio Frio and San Miguel River, a dozen miles into Texas territory. "They should be about here by now. Twenty-five, maybe thirty, miles from us. I think they've got San Antonio in mind."

Karnes mouthed a curse. Every officer in the Mexican Army wanted to make his reputation with San Antonio. The city was more than a strategic point. It was a matter of national pride.

"Artillery?"

"No."

"That cuts the odds," Karnes muttered as much to himself as to Jack. Karnes refolded the map. Jack knew the colonel wouldn't need to refer to it again. One glance was enough. Karnes fell silent, staring toward the range of rolling hills to the south.

Jack chewed on the venison. In San Antonio it would have been considered overcooked and stringy. Out here it was better than prime steak broiled over mesquite coals.

"Any chance they saw you, Jack?"

Jack spat out a small piece of gristle. "I don't think so. After I sized up their camp, I followed them for about four hours to make sure of their route. Figured by then I had about used up my luck, so Judas and I put some ground between us and them."

Karnes waved the other Rangers to the camp fire, then turned again to Jack. "You'll need a fresh horse. Take the blue roan from the pack string. He's got plenty of speed and he's been in a fight before. You can trust him."

By the time Jack had switched his Mexican-made saddle from Judas to the roan, the Ranger company was ready to move. Breakfast would be a handful of *panolin,* a mixture of parched corn, bear fat and thick, heavy syrup, sun-dried to be eaten on horseback and washed down with a swig of canteen water. Jack mounted the roan and let his gaze drift about the Ranger unit. Twenty-eight men, counting himself, against seventy Mexicans— fifty lancers and twenty mounted infantry called dragoons. Nobody had questioned the odds.

The Texans were a tough-looking bunch, Jack conceded. Each

man was armed with a pair of horse pistols, long rifle or shotgun, with knives, powderhorns and patch-and-ball pouches at their belts. They would never pass parade muster in the regular army. They were an unwashed, bearded lot, with no semblance of uniforms. Their clothing ranged from the once-fine black silk suit worn by a physician-Ranger named Robinson to the greasy buckskins and tough knee-high moccasins of former teamster Bill Williams. Doc Robinson always wore a string tie and white shirt, even in the field, and a wad of tobacco the size of a horse apple stretched his jaw out of shape. The distended cheek reminded Jack of Bigfoot Wallace. He missed the big frontiersman's company as well as his rifle. But Wallace was off somewhere along the Red River, scouting for another survey crew. *Too bad, Bigfoot,* Jack thought, *you could have settled a few debts with Mexicans here today.*

Karnes silently waved a hand and the company kneed their horses into motion. Jack rode at Karnes's side at the head of the column, the private and the colonel stirrup to stirrup. Differences in rank meant nothing to a Ranger company in the field.

Six hours later, Karnes, Jack Hays and Doc Robinson lay belly-down on a ridge overlooking a shallow swale.

"Damned if they're not a pretty sight," Karnes said.

A half-mile below, the Mexican lancers rode in sharp formation by the two's, red and blue uniforms bright against tall grass crisped to a dun color by a late-season drought. Sunlight danced on polished buttons and lance heads. The Mexican flag fluttered in the breeze, crackling above the gold braid and heavy epaulettes of the Mexican captain's uniform. Jack's estimation of their route and speed of travel had been on target. The Mexican force was within a half hour's ride of where his guess had placed them.

At his back, Jack heard the soft snuffle of horses, the creak of saddle leather and rustle of equipment as the Ranger company made a final check of their weapons.

"Plan to parley with them, Colonel?" Robinson asked, his voice low.

Karnes snorted. "Parley, hell. They know damn well they're on the soil of the sovereign nation of Texas. We'll just invite them back where they belong." The Ranger colonel brushed a small black spider from his shirt sleeve. "Let's go dirty up some pretty uniforms, Jack," he said. "You take the second platoon. I'll take the first."

Jack watched and waited as the lancers neared the Ranger ambush. With him were ten men, jaws clenched beneath their beards and suntans. Henry Karnes's platoon of ten waited patiently at the top of the rise, long rifles cocked and ready. To the rear, Doc Robinson and two more Rangers guarded the horses. Bill Williams and the remaining Texans, the best riflemen in the group, were stationed in rocky outcrops along the flanks, where they would have a clear field of fire for sharpshooting.

Jack glanced at the young private at his side. Mickey MacDonough, barely as tall as his German-made rifle, calmly licked a thumb and wiped the trace of spittle over the front blade sight of his battle-scarred weapon.

"Give 'em hell, men!"

Karnes's call triggered a volley from the riflemen in the first platoon. Three Mexicans tumbled from saddles in the first crack of Texas rifles; a fourth went down with his horse as a heavy ball slammed into the animal's chest. The shock of the unexpected attack momentarily disorganized the lancers. Jack led his men over the crest of the ridge. Karnes's riflemen were already beginning to reload.

Jack sprinted another ten yards, then dropped to one knee. He shouldered his rifle, swung the muzzle toward a lancer barely fifty yards away, pulled the trigger and grimaced in disgust as the ball missed its target. Nine other rifles belched blue-gray smoke, emptying two more Mexican saddles. Jack's hands moved without thought as he reloaded: powder charge down the muzzle, patch and ball down, ram, pull and store ramrod, lift hammer, flip away spent cap, put new cap on nipple, shoulder rifle, aim, fire.

He heard the shouts of the Mexican officer above the bellow of the Ranger rifles and the more distant crack of the Texas sharpshooters' long guns. The wavering Mexican ranks firmed. The lancers, the Mexican Army's best horsemen, kneed their mounts into two skirmish lines. The dragoons dismounted to fight on foot, firing toward the Rangers. A ball spat dirt near Jack's knee. He forced himself to take a slow breath, hold and squeeze. The rifle bucked against his shoulder and a Mexican went down. The remaining lancers slammed spurs into their mounts.

The first charge crumpled beneath the pounding of the Texans' guns. Jack dropped his rifle and pulled the two horse pistols from his waistband. The second wave of lancers tore through the gathering dust and smoke. Jack fired as a rider swept past, then spun to face the point of a lance in another Mexican's hand. He dove to his right, away from the lance, rolled to his knees and fired his second pistol into the lancer's back.

The battle closed to hand-to-hand combat, Mexican sword and lance against Texan knives and clubbed guns. Jack dodged a sword slash from an unhorsed Mexican, ripped his pistol barrel across the man's face and felt bones crumple beneath the blow. The Mexican fell. At Jack's side, Mickey MacDonough calmly sidestepped a lancer's charge, raised his rifle and aimed with care. The weapon roared almost in Jack's ear; at the corner of his field of vision Jack saw the Mexican officer straighten in the saddle, then slump to the side and fall. Jack heard MacDonough's grunt of surprise. He glanced toward the Ranger, saw MacDonough stagger and go down, a stain spreading on his shirt.

The Mexican ranks wavered once more, then broke. Horsemen wheeled mounts and raced away from the battlefield, followed by men on foot. Jack knew the battle was now a rout. The Mexicans, drilled day after day to follow commands until obedience was an instinct, were helpless without a commanding officer.

Moments later the Texans had remounted and were riding down stragglers from the shattered Mexican column. "Keep the pressure on!" Karnes called. "Run 'em back to Mexico!"

The pursuit, broken by sporadic gunshots and the occasional clang of steel on steel, continued through mid-afternoon until the last of the battered lancer force splashed through the shallow Nueces onto Mexican soil.

The sun rode low in the western sky when Karnes's Rangers returned to the original battle site with three lancers wounded and nine pale but otherwise healthy captives in tow. Doc Robinson met the party a hundred yards from the battleground. His boiled shirt was streaked in blood.

"How do we stand, Doc?" Karnes asked by way of greeting.

"MacDonough's dead. Jackson, Maguire and Kirby were hurt. Jackson caught a slug in the calf. Kirby got a lance in the shoulder. Maguire's pistol blew up on him, broke his hand and took off a chunk of scalp. Pieces missed his eyes. They'll all live if they don't get blood poisoning." Doc Robinson pulled a tobacco plug from his shirt pocket. His nose wrinkled in distaste. The quid was soiled by blood.

Karnes pulled his own tobacco twist from his "possibles" pouch and tossed it to Robinson. "The Mexicans?" he asked.

Robinson shrugged. "Seven dead here. Two more won't see sunup. We've got a dozen or so prisoners."

"We killed four more by my count between here and the river," Karnes said. He stabbed a thumb toward the injured lancers. "When you get the notion, Doc, see what you can do for the Mexicans. No hurry."

Doc Robinson raised an eyebrow. "We going to shoot them, Colonel? No use wasting time and our supplies patching them up if we are."

"No. We won't shoot them." Karnes let his gaze drift over the captive Mexicans. The lancers' heads were bowed, shoulders slumped. They did not struggle against their ropes. "They might come in handy for a prisoner swap. A sorry lot they are, but they might at least be worth a couple of Texans, should the need arise. Patch them up, Doc, and let's head back to San Antonio."

THREE

San Antonio
November 1839

An early-season norther with more bluster than bite nosed against the livery stable behind San Antonio's Catholic church, sniffing out cracks in the adobe and stone structure. The rise and fall of the wind muffled the chant of the priest as he blessed the combatants glaring at each other across the clean-swept dirt square.

Jack Hays leaned against the top rail of a stall at the rear of the crowd and listened as the priest completed the blessing. *With all the problems facing the Creator,* Jack wondered, *would a Supreme Being really care about the outcome of a rooster fight?* A murmur swept the gathering and quickly grew to a clamor as bettors called out their wagers. The crowd was mostly a sea of brown, with an Anglo face providing a white breaker here and there against the torrent of excited Mexican voices.

"Putting a bet down on this one, Jack?" Colonel Henry Karnes shouldered his way through the crowd, trailed by a big man with a tobacco-stained beard. Karnes idly thumbed a thick stack of Mexican silver.

"No, Colonel," Jack said. "Looks like you did well on the last bird, though."

Karnes grinned. "Noticed the priest heeled the left spur crooked on the big bird. They fought that rooster last week.

Looked to me like he fought left-handed. Or maybe left-footed would be a more accurate way to say it. The little rooster had straight spurs and a mean look in his eye. So I put a few pesos on him." Karnes gestured to the big man at his side. "Bill Davis, meet Jack Hays."

Jack's hand all but disappeared in Davis's grip. The big man's grin was genuine, a flash of surprisingly white teeth against sun-browned skin. Shoulder-length hair tumbled from beneath a travel-stained bowler hat. "Heard about you, Jack Hays," Davis said. "Pleasure to meet you."

"Bill's joining our little group," Karnes said. "He's a heller with a long rifle and not half bad with a Bowie knife." Karnes waved a hand, called out a bet on the red rooster in Spanish and acknowledged two immediate replies. "Bill helped clean up the Cherokee problems in East Texas this summer. Served under Ed Burleson in the militia."

Jack saluted Davis's service with a nod. He hadn't personally agreed with the campaign against Chief Bowles and the Cherokees, but it had been necessary. The Mexicans had been courting the Cherokees, hoping to use them as a weapon against the Texans. Documents and letters taken from two dead Mexicans in different skirmishes had detailed the plan. There were now rumors the Mexicans were flirting with the Comanches for the same reason.

"Glad to have you with us, Bill," Jack said. "We can use a man with some experience."

"Comanche's a different animal from a Cherokee," Karnes said. "Thought you might sort of take Bill under your wing, Jack. Got to warn you, though. He's a little wild."

In the ring, the two handlers teased their birds into a feathered fury as the final bets went down, then released the fighters. The roar of the crowd put a momentary end to any further conversation.

Jack Hays paid no attention to the progress of the rooster fight. He studied the faces in the crowd. The Sunday cockfights and the occasional *baile,* or fandango, were the chief forms of entertainment in San Antonio, drawing Mexican and Texan together for a common break in the tedium of daily existence. On these occasions, it seemed, there was no show of tension or suspicion on either side. Mexican and Anglo alike honored their bets. Few people of either race went armed to such social events. Jack found it a curiosity, one of the fascinating quirks of Texas frontier life.

Colonel Karnes's red rooster went down, its breast pierced by a sharp steel shaft. Karnes groaned in disgust and paid off his bets.

A Mexican prostitute working the crowd pushed an ample breast against Jack's arm. *"Pechos grandes, señor,"* she said. *"No calzones. Diez pesos."*

Jack smiled and shook his head. "Not today, señorita." The woman sighed and pushed away.

"What did she say?" Bill Davis's thick brows arched as he watched the sway of the woman's hips.

Karnes laughed. "Your first lesson in border Mexican, Bill," he said. "She said she had big breasts, wore no underpants, and her price was ten pesos."

Davis glanced at Jack. Mischief twinkled in the brown eyes. "You need a loan, Mister Hays, I've got the ten pesos."

Jack grinned. "Thanks for the offer, but today I'm not in the market."

The conversation ended abruptly as Bill Williams shoved through the crowd to Karnes's side. The lanky frontiersman bore the look and smell of a hard ride.

"Colonel, I think we got us some trouble," Williams said, ignoring the formalities of greeting. "I cut sign of a dozen Mexican carts headed north toward Verde Creek. Loaded heavy and off the main trails. Don't like the look of it."

"Comancheros?"

"That's my guess," Williams said. "Canales has been trying to get guns to the Comanches. No other reason for *carretas* out there. Unless they're collectin' prickly pear, and there's plenty of that in Mexico."

Karnes's frown deepened. "Damn that Canales's bones. The only edge we have on the Comanches is they don't have many guns, and the old Chaparral Fox knows it. Grab a fresh horse, Williams. Jack, gather up all the Rangers you can find. We ride in twenty minutes. Davis, you want to come along? Your enlistment isn't official until tomorrow.''

Davis grinned. ''Might as well.'' He gazed toward the Mexican whore who had sidled up to the big winner in the last round of cockfight betting. ''Probably save me ten pesos, anyway.''

Jack Hays, rifle nested in the crook of an elbow, stood beside Henry Karnes in a bend of the narrow trail which wound between the low hills south of Verde Creek. Karnes leaned against his own rifle, hands crossed casually over the muzzle, his gaze steady on the swarthy face of the man in the lead cart. Eleven other mule-drawn *carretas* draped in gum sheets were bunched close behind. The drivers walked alongside the carts, weapons in hand or within easy reach.

''Eh, *amigo*,'' the man in the lead cart called, ''why do you stand in our way? The road is narrow here.''

''Sorry, friend,'' Karnes replied in Spanish. ''I can't let you through until I check your cargo.''

The swarthy one's face split in a crooked grin. He swung the muzzle of a heavy pistol toward Karnes. ''And who would dare to search the carts of Juan Estaval? A man should know the name of the one he is about to kill.''

''Colonel Henry Karnes, Texas Rangers, Juan Estaval.'' Karnes smiled politely. ''I do not think you will kill me. It would be unwise.''

Estaval's laugh was the cackle of a goose. ''Unwise? What would you do, Henry Karnes? Place a curse upon this poor peon's bones from the grave?''

Karnes shrugged. ''From your own grave. Kill me, my friend here kills you. Or perhaps one of *his* friends. Look about you, Estaval.''

The Mexican glanced to one side of the road, then the other. Texas Rangers stood at the crest of the low hills on each side, rifles and shotguns trained on the teamsters. Estaval's face paled. He reluctantly lowered his pistol and forced a nervous smile. ''Señor Karnes, I am but a poor merchant trying to earn an honest living.'' The brash confidence was gone from his tone. ''I am merely a trader. I have goods to exchange with your allies, the Lipans. I have a permit from the *alcalde* of Laredo himself to conduct such business."

"A permit from the *alcalde* of Laredo is worth about as much as a lizard fart on Texas soil." Karnes spat to emphasize the statement. "If your goods are legitimate, there will be no problem." He stared into Estaval's face. "There are no Lipans here. Only Paneteka Comanches. Perhaps you have taken the wrong trail. In any event, an honest trader such as yourself should have no objections to a search of the wagons."

"If I should object?"

"My friend here will shoot you."

For a moment Jack felt the heavy tension in the cool late autumn air and thought the Mexican might actually try to use the handgun. Hate flared in Estaval's eyes. Karnes continued to ignore the pistol. "The decision is yours, Estaval. Ask your companions if they would die with you."

The Mexican teamsters grounded their weapons and stepped back, hands raised. Karnes strode past Estaval to the lead wagon, untied the rope holding the gum sheet in place and flipped the covering away. The cart held powder, lead, a half-dozen aging muskets and three *escopetas,* the bell-barreled flintlock smoothbores popular with Mexican ranchers and their *vaqueros.*

Jack struggled to control his growing anger as Karnes finished the inspection. Each cart contained guns, ammunition, knives, several jugs of mescal and bottles of tequila. Karnes kept his pace measured as he walked back to Estaval.

"Supplying guns to Comanches is a serious offense in Texas, Estaval. You are not, at this moment, a popular man." Karnes leaned against the high wheel of the cart and glared at the Mexican. "Estaval," he said, his voice tight with anger, "it took a lot of money to put this shipment together. Who supplied that money?"

The Mexican's only reply was a curse.

"Have it your way, Estaval. Jack, shoot the bastard."

Jack raised his rifle and lined the sights on Estaval's forehead. His finger tightened on the trigger until he felt the delicate balance of the sear against the hammer release.

The Mexican's nerve broke.

"Canales." Estaval's voice was a husky croak. His wide-eyed

gaze was fixed on the muzzle of Jack's rifle. "In the name of God, it was Canales."

"That's a beginning, Estaval. Now the rest. Other names, places. What Comanche band you were to meet and where."

Jack lowered the rifle. Estaval talked for five minutes. Henry Karnes listened with care, occasionally jotting a name or a place in a small notebook. "That's all I know," Estaval concluded, his tone pleading. "For God's sake, Colonel—don't shoot me."

Karnes shrugged in dismissal. "We won't shoot you here, Estaval. Maybe later we will hang you, maybe not. *¿Quién sabe?* For now, you and your men are our prisoners." The Ranger colonel turned his back on Estaval. "Jack, there are some Comanches up ahead waiting for guns. What do you think about the situation?"

"I think we might as well give them some guns. At least the part that comes out the end of the barrel."

"Mister Hays," Karnes said, suddenly jovial, "you are a man of infinite wisdom. I was thinking the same thing. Now, let's get these prisoners trussed up. We'll leave a couple of men here to guard them. We'll burn the carts on the way back, after we kick a few Comanches in the *cojones.*"

Buzzards milled above the mile-wide prairie flat at the headwaters of Verde Creek, tattered wings locked to soar with the freshening breeze or flapping laboriously on the upwind tack over the Comanche camp. Jack had learned to read the buzzards. The big birds always followed a large Indian band. The more Comanches, the more buzzards. There were a lot of birds overhead today.

Jack reined Judas to the left, taking his place in the staggered double skirmish line of Rangers, with Bill Davis at his side. There was no opportunity for an ambush. This would be a straight, flat-out fight. Eighteen Texans on tiring horses against about fifty well-mounted Indians.

Most of the Comanches already were mounted and riding toward the Texans, arrows nocked and ready, spears held aloft. Lowering gray clouds hid the sun, casting an eerie pall of colorless half-light over the battleground. The Indians pulled their mounts to a halt. For a few moments, Comanche and Texan faced each other across a frost-brittle sea of grass.

"Damn," Bill Davis said in awe, "there must be a hundred of them out there."

"More like half that many," Jack said. "Out here, that's about as close to even as it ever gets for us."

"What are they waiting for?"

"Didn't expect to see us. Comanches don't like surprises."

One of the Comanches yipped, a high-pitched trill that reminded Jack of a stuttering coyote. From somewhere in the Ranger ranks came an answering Texas war cry.

The Rangers surged forward, driving steel to their mounts. Comanches quirted ponies toward the Texans. The distance between the two lines of horsemen closed rapidly.

"Dismount and fire!"

At Karnes's call, the Texans slid their horses to a stop, knelt and brought rifles to full cock. A half-dozen Comanches outraced the rest, charged into rifle range and slipped down the side of their horses, arms looped through handholds braided into the ponies' manes. Arrows whipped from beneath the ponies' necks toward the Texans. Most fell short; one shaft struck a stone ten feet in front of Jack as he squeezed the trigger. A Comanche pony staggered. Its legs collapsed. The rider kicked free of the falling mount and landed on his feet. Another warrior raced forward, leaned from his horse, looped arms with the downed brave and swung him onto the horse's rump without breaking stride.

Bill Davis rammed a fresh charge down his rifle barrel as he watched. "Damn me if those red devils can't ride," he yelled over the crack of weapons.

The battle settled into a grim routine, the Texans alternately firing, reloading and resuming the charge, the Indians swooping in to loose arrows or lances, always on the move. The Comanches slowly gave ground under the superior firepower of the Texans, a dozen of them keeping the Rangers busy as the remainder of the band whipped horses across the creek toward the safety of the broken hills to the north.

An hour later, the Verde Creek fight was over. Four Comanches lay dead on the battlefield. Two more were down along the creek, victims of the Texas long rifles. Bill Davis dropped one fleeing Indian from three hundred yards, a shot that brought a murmur of respect from the Ranger ranks.

The Texans' pursuit of the Indians lasted little more than two miles before Karnes waved the Rangers to a halt. "We're wasting our time chasing them," Karnes said. "They've got fresh mounts and our horses are worn out. We might as well go home."

A pillar of smoke lay flat on the north wind as Karnes led his company of Rangers away from the Verde Creek battleground. Jack knew the raid was a success despite the few Comanches killed. The Indians had been forced to abandon most of their trade goods, food and blankets. What the Texans couldn't use from the plunder they put to the torch. Five Rangers herded more than twenty Indian horses taken in the raid. In Indian terms, this particular band of Comanches was now as poor as a Sonoran shepherd and winter was coming on.

Karnes let his horse drop back alongside Jack's mount.

"Why the frown, Jack? Seems like we had a pretty good couple of days."

Jack tugged his coat snug against the growing bite of the wind. "I was just thinking. There's got to be a better way to fight Indians. Mexicans, too."

Karnes raised an eyebrow. "I'd welcome your ideas."

Jack twisted in the saddle to look Karnes in the eye. "Colonel, we need more of an edge. Everywhere we turn, we're outnumbered. The Indians and the Mexicans are the finest horsemen I've ever seen, and they can fight from horseback. We have to fight on foot. A good Comanche warrior can put six, eight arrows in the air while we're firing once and reloading. If we just had some way to stay mounted, something besides single-shot weapons, it would even the odds."

Karnes pulled his quid from his pouch and gnawed off a substantial chew, brows bunched in thought. "Can't argue with that point. As of now, we're mounted infantry." The colonel's gaze drifted along the line of Rangers. They had been in the saddle for twenty hours and had covered more than a hundred miles, captured a Comanchero cart train and dealt the Comanches a serious blow. And not a one of them looked tired. Dirty, maybe, but not tired. "These are good men. They deserve more. I wish I had an answer for you, Jack."

San Antonio
January 1840

Jack Hays sat in a straight-backed rawhide chair across from Colonel Henry Karnes and nursed a cup of strong black coffee. The fireplace crackled against the low moan of the sharp winter wind. For the first time in two weeks Jack was beginning to feel warm.

"Sorry to call you in less than an hour after a long patrol, Jack," Karnes said.

Jack grinned ruefully. "That's how I earn my dollar and a quarter a day, Colonel." He tried not to let his concern for his commanding officer show. Henry Karnes's normally florid face was pale, the eyes sunken and dull. He had lost weight and his handshake was only a shadow of the powerful grip of a month ago. He hadn't ridden a patrol since the Verde Creek fight.

"How did it go out there?"

"Froze our butts in a cold rain, with a little sleet thrown in for variety, for thirteen days," Jack said. "Covered two hundred miles and didn't cut a single track, Indian or Mexican. No sign of Canales or any of his gunrunners, and I'm dead certain Estaval and the other two Comancheros we caught last month weren't the only cards in Canales's deck. It's all quiet along the Nueces. For now, at least. I'll have a full report for you tomorrow."

Karnes fished the coffee pot from its brace over the fire and refilled Jack's cup. His hands trembled. "Jack, I didn't really ask you here for a report on your patrol. I'll get right to the hooves and horns of this critter. The Comanches have asked for a meeting. They say they want to talk peace."

"Peace talks? That doesn't sound like our Comanches."

"I don't know. Our ranging companies have kept a lot of pressure on them. We've disrupted their summer and fall hunts, cost them more than a few warriors. There's been a lot of wailing in Comanche strongholds this year. They've had to cut back on raids because of our patrols. I think they may be getting a bit

worried about how they're going to feed their women and kids."
Karnes paused for a sip of coffee, then flashed a weak grin at
Jack. "You might be interested that the Comanches have hung a
name on you, Jack. Powerful Water."

Jack raised an eyebrow. "What?"

Karnes chuckled. "Well, that's the more delicate translation.
Literally, you're now 'Big Pisser' to the Paneteka. Quite a compli-
mentary name, to a Comanche."

The smile faded from the colonel's face as quickly as it had
formed. "Maybe we've got them in a bind and maybe not. I'm
not sure we've hurt them all that much." Karnes plucked a pen
from the clutter on his desk and twirled the staff in his fingers.
"Three of the chiefs came to me while you were out on patrol. I
told them there would be no talks unless they turned over all the
captives they now hold."

"They agreed?"

"Yes." Karnes tapped the pen staff on the edge of the desk.
"What do you make of it, Jack? You've come to know these Indians as well as I do."

Jack paused, scratched an itch along his bearded jaw as he
thought. "I don't like the sound of it, Colonel. The Comanches
are in winter camp now. They can't do much hunting or raiding
until the grass comes in the spring and fattens their ponies.
Maybe they're just buying time until the Comanche Moon."

"That's what has me worried." Karnes nibbled at the end of
the pen staff. "On the other hand, we can't pass up a chance at
getting our people back. I don't trust the Comanches, Jack. I've
been down this peace talk road with them before. A Comanche
will look you straight in the eye, tell you the moon is black,
expect you to believe it and wait for you to give him a present for
his wisdom. They've broken every peace treaty we've made with
them." Karnes tossed the pen staff back into the paper clutter of
the desk. "The parley's been called for March, at the Council
House here. I would like you to be at that meeting, as my repre-
sentative. This damn fever's dragged me down until I couldn't
pull a sick whore off a chamber pot."

Even the effort of talking seemed to tire Karnes. Weariness was
heavy in his voice. "I've got to go to Houston, maybe even New
Orleans," he said, "and I want someone whose judgment I trust

at the parley." Karnes leaned back in his chair and sighed heavily. "I've written the secretary of war, asking for help from the militia. But technically I'm regular Army myself, Jack, and I know how the 'official' reports get twisted to advance some officer's career. I want to know what *really* happens at that peace parley. In straight talk. Can I count on you?"

"Of course, Colonel." Jack drained the last of the coffee, sloshed the cup in a basin of water and replaced it on the mantel.

Karnes plucked a folded paper from atop the desk and handed it to Jack with trembling fingers. "You can write me at this address to report on the peace talks. Or to ask a favor, or just say hello."

Jack tucked the paper into a shirt pocket. "I'll be in touch every chance I have, Colonel. You take care of yourself. We need you out here." Jack reached for his hat.

"There's something else, Jack." Karnes's voice was noticeably weaker. "I'm putting you in command of the Ranger company here, as sergeant. I've already talked to the others about it. They trust you to keep their *cojones* intact for them."

"Colonel, I don't know about that; there are others with more experience—"

Karnes cut off Jack's objection with a wave of the hand. "You're a leader, Jack. Born to the job. Knew it from the first time I saw you in action. I'd like you to coordinate your efforts here with Matthew Caldwell in Gonzales. Old Paint's a top man. He'll be at the Council House for the parley. You have any questions, just ask Matthew."

Jack hesitated, then nodded. Old Paint Caldwell was a veteran Indian fighter, a leader respected throughout Texas for his courage and ability in the field. "I'll work with Caldwell," he said, "and do my best until you get back."

"I may not be back this time. Now, Jack Hays, clear out of my office. I don't like good-byes. Keep your hair on at the Council House. And keep that damned Canales and his like out of San Antonio."

FOUR

San Antonio
March 1840

Jack Hays leaned against the rough stone wall of the dirt-floored Council House, the one-story building at the corner of Main Plaza and Calaboza Street. He surveyed the gathering and was not pleased with what he saw. More than forty Comanche warriors and a dozen powerful chiefs stood in the crowded interior, facing the low wooden table and rough-hewn bench where the peace commissioners sat.

Militia Colonel William G. Cooke and Adjutant General Hugh McLeod presided at the direction of President Lamar. Lieutenant Colonel William S. Fisher, commander of the First Regiment of Infantry, sat alongside the commissioners.

Outside, Indian women and children waited in the courtyard. The youngsters amused themselves with games and displays of bow-and-arrow prowess as a crowd of white men and women watched, drawn to the spectacle of a major peace parley. Also outside were three companies of Fisher's infantry, sent in response to Henry Karnes's plea for military help, and Captain Tom Howard's company of Texas Rangers. At Caldwell's suggestion Jack had sent his own company to prowl the Nueces. It was rumored that Canales was in the area.

Jack glanced across the room to where Howard and Old Paint

stood alongside troopers stationed at the main door to the court-yard. Caldwell's answering glance told Jack the veteran Indian fighter shared his worry. Aside from the three Rangers, practically no one in the building understood the Comanches. McLeod knew something of Indians, but not Comanches. A man didn't need a New Orleans fortune teller to see trouble ahead, Jack thought. Lamar's instructions to Fisher had set an ominous tone even before the meeting—if the Comanches did not produce the scores of white captives believed held, the Indian chiefs were to be arrested and held as hostages. Jack knew a Comanche warrior would never surrender under these circumstances. Also, on Lamar's orders, there had been no gifts for the Indians, a serious breach of protocol. The chiefs had been surly to begin with. The lack of gifts had only worsened their temperament.

Jack wished he had brought a pistol. He was armed only with his belt knife, as were Howard and Caldwell. The Indians carried knives, axes, bows and arrows, and one held a lance from which dangled two scalps. The Comanche bows were strung. Traces of war paint still showed on several deep-copper faces. A bad sign. Jack could almost taste the tension in the heavy air of the poorly ventilated Council House.

Half Hand was among the Comanche band. His dark eyes glittered with hate and seldom strayed from Jack's face. The Indian had not forgotten the beating a simple survey party had dealt his band in the Sacramento foothills, or the man responsible for it. Half Hand's left shoulder still drooped from the wound inflicted by Bigfoot Wallace's rifle.

Jack dismissed Half Hand from his mind and turned his attention to the talks. He was within easy earshot of the council table from his post against the wall.

Muk-war-rah, the bald peace chief and most influential medicine man of the Paneteka band, served as spokesman for the Comanches. Muk-war-rah had just recited the list of Indian demands of ransom for the prisoners—blankets, cloth, vermilion, knives, one hundred horses, thirty rifles and powder and ball "for hunting." Now the medicine man stood defiantly awaiting McLeod's reply.

McLeod fixed a steady gaze on Muk-war-rah. "There will be no goods and no further talk of peace until you have delivered the white prisoners as promised," McLeod said.

Muk-war-rah waved a hand.

A single white girl, thin to the point of starvation, stumbled from the Indian ranks. She stood before the commissioners, head bowed, shoulders trembling. The girl's appearance sent a shocked silence through the white men present. Her body was scarred, purpled by bruises and speckled by weeping sores. The flesh of her nose was burned away to the bone. Only a scabbed, gaping hole remained where her nostrils had been.

The stunned quiet gave way to a low murmur of outrage among the Texans. Jack Hays felt his own belly churn. One of the Comanche ideas of great fun was to place burning coals on the body of a sleeping captive.

"Here is your prisoner." Muk-war-rah's tone was heavy with contempt.

McLeod ignored the medicine man. "What is your name, child?"

"Matilda, sir. Matilda Lockhart."

"Come to me, Matilda." The commissioner stood, put his arm around the girl's thin shoulders. The two talked softly for several minutes. McLeod gestured to a trooper standing nearby. "Take this poor child to someone who can ease her pain." He stroked the girl's dirty, tangled hair in a fatherly gesture. "They won't hurt you anymore, Matilda."

McLeod waited until the trooper and the girl had left, then abruptly wheeled to face the medicine man. "Where are the other prisoners you promised to bring, Muk-war-rah?" McLeod's voice trembled in fury.

"We have brought the only one we had. The others are with other tribes."

The commissioner made no reply. He pinned an icy stare on the bald Indian. The tension grew with each heartbeat, became a living thing in the crowded room. Muk-war-rah and the other Comanche leaders stood in mute defiance, their bearing mocking the Texans. Muk-war-rah was the one who finally broke the silence. "How do you like that answer?"

McLeod nodded a silent signal to Colonel Fisher. Within seconds a company of Fisher's men marched into the Council

House and took up posts along the walls, rifles at the ready. Jack let his hand drop to the knife at his belt. The place was a powder keg with a live coal on top.

"The girl you abused and tortured was not of simple mind, Muk-war-rah," McLeod said. "She learned enough of your language to tell me something. That she had seen many other white prisoners in the Comanche camps. That she overheard your plans to bring them to us one at a time in order to drive up the price."

Muk-war-rah sniffed in disdain. "You are lucky to get the one. We will bring you the others, but first you will grant our demands."

McLeod leaned forward, rage coloring his cheeks. "I do not trust Muk-war-rah. The Comanches have broken previous pledges to surrender captives and live in peace. I have no reason to believe you are not lying to us once more."

Muk-war-rah's body stiffened at the insult, but the sneer of contempt remained on his face. "We have made our offer. You may take it, or leave it and see the white man swept from this land. As many of you will die as there are stars in the sky. Your women will provide amusement for Comanche warriors."

Jack Hays drew a slow, deep breath. *The insolent bastard has just cut his own throat,* he thought, *and maybe ours as well.* Jack felt the familiar relaxed, alert calm drape itself over his body. He glanced at Half Hand. The Paneteka subchief had edged through the crowd until he was only a few feet from Jack. The Indian's good hand rested on the haft of a butcher knife at his hip.

"Muk-war-rah," McLeod said, his voice quavering in anger, "you and your companions are now our prisoners. You will be jailed here until all white captives held by the Comanches have been delivered."

The metallic *click* of hammers drawn to full cock on soldiers' rifles seemed to echo in the Council House.

"Put down your weapons and surrender," McLeod demanded.

An Indian yelled and sprang toward the front door. Steel flashed as the Comanche drove the blade of his knife into Tom Howard's side. An Army sentinel fired his rifle point-blank into the Indian's body. The Council House erupted in a frenzy of gunshots, the thud of bodies crashing together in combat and the yelps of Comanche and Texan.

Half Hand hurled himself toward Jack, the heavy butcher knife at shoulder level. Jack whipped his own knife from its sheath and pushed away from the wall to meet Half Hand. The Comanche swung the butcher knife as if it were a sword, but Jack deflected the blow with a forearm, stepped in close and ripped his own blade upward. The keen tip slid in below Half Hand's ribs. The blade tore upward into the Comanche's heart. Jack twisted the knife, then yanked it free, face to face with Half Hand. The Indian gasped once and sagged, black eyes already beginning to glaze. Jack hurled the dying Comanche aside and threw himself into the hand-to-hand battle that raged through the Council House.

Over the screams of the wounded and dying, Jack heard the crack of rifles and deeper cough of shotguns outside the meeting house. He knew the Indians who had fought their way from the building were being cut down by Texas guns in the hands of Rangers and militiamen.

The battle surged toward the door, sweeping Jack along as he grappled with a big, broad-shouldered Comanche. Jack found an opening, rammed a knee into the Indian's groin and ripped his knife across the back of the man's neck. The Indian grunted and fell. Jack caught a quick glimpse of Matthew Caldwell, blood streaming from a leg wound as he swung the stock of a soldier's gun into the face of a Comanche. The bloody battle spilled into the courtyard. Jack stumbled over a body. A Comanche pulled his bow, the arrow pointing at Jack's heart, then spun and fell as a rifle ball tore away his throat. The arrow fluttered harmlessly to the ground.

A half hour later Jack Hays, blood-spattered but uninjured, stood outside the Council House and surveyed the carnage. Seven Texans had died and eight were wounded. Thirty-three Indians, including most of the chiefs and the bald medicine man Muk-war-rah, lay dead. Thirty-two Indian prisoners huddled in a glum knot before Texas rifles. Jack knew the Comanches expected to be killed, as they themselves killed prisoners. They awaited their fate in stoic silence.

In addition to the Indian captives, the Texans held more than a hundred Comanche horses, a substantial pile of buffalo robes, animal pelts and captured weapons.

Gunfire in the streets of San Antonio slowed to an occasional shot as soldiers and residents dispatched Indians who had escaped the initial battle. The Council House fight was over. And with it, Jack knew, any slim chance of peace with the Comanches. A few feet from Jack, General McLeod called Lieutenant Colonel Fisher to his side. Fisher's own uniform was torn, the blade of his sword stained. Blood seeped from a small nick on Fisher's chin.

"Pick one Comanche woman from the captives," McLeod said. "Put her on a good horse. Tell her to ride to the tribes and tell them what happened here. She is to inform them that no Comanche prisoners will be freed until all white captives are returned to us here. *All* white captives. Make sure she understands the Indians have fourteen days to comply, or we will kill the hostages." Fisher moved away to do the commissioner's bidding.

McLeod turned to Jack. "Mister Hays, you know these people well, I'm told. How soon do you expect them to meet our demands for a prisoner exchange?"

Jack grimaced. He fought back the urge to swing a fist into the peace commissioner's face. "General McLeod," he said bitterly, "they won't. You've signed the death warrant for a lot of white captives here today and we're still going to be up to our butts in Indians. Now and for fifty years to come."

Jack spun on a heel and made his way to Old Paint Caldwell's side. An errant ball from a soldier's rifle had struck Caldwell in the leg. The wound was bloody, but didn't appear serious. Ranger Captain Tom Howard was in worse shape. The blade had gone deep into his side. Jack had no way of knowing if the knife had sliced into his gut. If it had, Tom Howard faced a long and painful death. If it hadn't, he might live. Jack helped Caldwell stop the blood flow and bind the leg wound, then assisted him to his feet. Rangers from Howard's company, faces grim and grimy from the battle, gathered around their wounded leader.

Old Paint tested the leg and winced. "Smarts a tad, but it'll mend. Lend me a shoulder over to the Mavericks' house. Mary Maverick's a better doctor than any of these Army butchers. I'm out of the saddle for a few days, Jack. Looks like it's up to you and your San Antonio boys to handle this hornet's nest, and I don't envy you the job.''

San Antonio
June 1840

Jack Hays dismounted in front of Sam Maverick's stable and rubbed his backside, numbed from almost three months of eighteen-hour days in the saddle.

Judas's head drooped at the hitch rail. The sorrel's flanks were gaunt, his sides and chest soaked by fresh sweat streaked with salty lather. Jack stripped the saddle and blanket, led the horse to a nearby water trough and let him drink for a minute before pulling his head up. Too much water too soon after a long ride could disable a horse for weeks, maybe even kill him. Jack reached for a piece of burlap and began rubbing Judas down. Jack had acquired two more mounts since the Council House fiasco. Both of them now looked as drawn-down as Judas.

The days had blurred, one into the other, under the monotony of the long scouts broken by the occasional sharp clash with small bands of Comanche raiders in which little damage was done to either side. Images flitted through Jack's mind. The gut-wrenching discovery of a lone traveler or family butchered by Comanches. The broiling heat of a rainless summer, streams and springs that normally carried fresh water now baked dry by the furnace heat and relentless wind that swept from the border desert across San Antonio into the Hill Country. Bone-crunching patrols along the Nueces, watching for signs of invasion from Mexico while the Western defenses of Texas were tied down with Indian trouble. The images held a mix of despair and elation. Elation when Mrs. James Webster and her three-year-old child escaped from a Comanche camp to the relative safety of San Antonio. Relief when Mrs. Webster's older son Booker was ransomed a few weeks later. Despair as young Booker described the agonized death of thirteen captives, bound to stakes or spits and roasted over slow fires, or skinned alive. Matilda Lockhart's younger sister was among the victims. That news had hurt.

Jack finished the rubdown, led Judas into a stall and dished out a double ration of grain. He leaned against the stall rail and listened to the crunch of grain as Judas ate. The sound was somehow reassuring, even if it did seem the horse's head must be void of brains, with the chewing noises just echoing around inside. The sorrel snorted from time to time, clearing grain dust from his nostrils.

The San Antonio Ranger group had had its share of disappointments of late, but two weeks ago Jack had gotten a personal boost of spirit; Bigfoot Wallace had intercepted them on the trail. "Heard you had a speck of Indian trouble," Wallace said. "Figured you could use a hand."

The militia infantry companies were no help, other than to possibly protect San Antonio from direct attack. Their only other contribution was guarding the Comanche prisoners, and they did that poorly. Singly and in pairs the Indians had escaped. A pitiful few had been exchanged for white captives. Now only a handful remained in custody at the San Jose Mission.

Jack's Rangers were San Antonio's only effective fighting force outside the town limits. While they weren't large in numbers, they were big in ability.

The core of the Ranger group were men tried and proven on the frontier. Bigfoot Wallace, whose propensity for tall tales and wry humor under fire was as legendary as the size of his moccasins. Bill Davis of the bowler hat, carefree, sometimes reckless, a crack shot with rifle and pistol and who drew women the way honey draws bears. Solemn Ben McCulloch, who seldom changed expression under fire but constantly battled to control a temper that lay just beneath the cold blue eyes. Samuel H. Walker, slight of build, sandy-haired, slump-shouldered, quiet to the point of shyness until the fight started, when he was always among the first in the charge and the last in the retreat. Bill Williams, the lanky, laconic frontiersman whose sharp eyes could turn a bent blade of grass into a map leading straight to an Indian camp.

There were men like Doc Robinson, the physician who could take a life as efficiently as he could save one; wiry Archibald

Gibson, whose slender build and penchant for quoting from classic literature belied the fighting ability of a cornered cougar; and Horace Rowe, who stood barely five-three and weighed almost a hundred-thirty pounds, author of a book of gentle verses, whose talents with a horse and gun were poetry in their own fashion.

Rounding out the force were seasoned frontiersmen, a few riders new to the Ranger game and civilian volunteers like San Antonio merchant Samuel Maverick, always among the first to answer the toll of the church bell calling men to arms. Maverick had proven his mettle in the field was equal to his efficiency behind a desk.

Jack knew he couldn't be riding with better men.

When Judas had finished the grain, Jack led him back to the water trough. This time it would be safe to let the sorrel drink all he wanted. The edge would be off the gelding's thirst. When the horse had his fill, Jack turned him into a corral behind the stables and started for the house, aware that he smelled worse than a Tonkawa blanket after a long winter. He wanted a bath and shave, but first he needed a parley with Old Paint. The last three patrols had been through empty land. It was quiet around San Antonio.

The silence was ominous.

Jack found Caldwell wiping an oiled rag over the barrel of a scarred Kentucky rifle in Sam Maverick's study. Old Paint put the weapon aside and listened intently as Jack made his report.

"Three hundred miles this time, from the Nueces to the Brazos," Jack concluded, "and not a Comanche in sight. Not a track or trail less than three weeks old."

Old Paint scratched the healing bullet wound in his leg. "Don't like the sound of it, Jack. Folks around here have started to relax. They think we've whipped the Comanches so bad the Indian troubles are over. That kind of thinking can get somebody killed. A lot of somebodies. How do you read all that empty country?"

Jack swabbed a hand through his hair. It came away covered in oily dirt and sweat. "Just a guess, Colonel, but I think the Comanches have pulled back northwest. Maybe as far as the Staked Plains, to mourn their dead, pick new leaders and fatten their ponies." Jack sighed and wiped the greasy palm over an equally dirty trouser leg. "Then I'm afraid we're in for a bad time, come the Comanche Moon."

Matthew Caldwell grunted his agreement. "I suspect you're right, Jack. We've got a bloodbath ahead of us, somewhere. I just hope to God we're both wrong."

Plum Creek
August 1840

"Dammit, Jack," Bigfoot Wallace said, "do you have to be right *all* the time?"

Jack Hays glanced at the big frontiersman. Bigfoot leaned against the trunk of a small tree, part of the timber and scrub brush lining the tributary of the San Marcos known as Plum Creek. Bigfoot's bulk threatened to permanently stunt the growth of the young oak. Jack swabbed his neckerchief at the sweat and trail grime on the back of his neck. "Lord knows I wanted to be wrong this time, Bigfoot," he said. "At least I didn't want to be *this* right."

Jack had called the Comanche raid almost to the day. During the first week in August, in the time of the Comanche Moon, a massive war party of nearly a thousand Indians, more than half of them warriors, struck deep into Texas.

Led by the Paneteka war chief Buffalo Hump, the Indians poured down the Guadalupe Valley, raided Victoria and drove on to sack and burn the small community of Linnville on the Texas coast. More than twenty Texans lay dead in the path of the marauders. A half-dozen more were captives, and now the Indians were headed back north to their home country with some two thousand stolen horses and more than a hundred pack mules carrying heavy loads of booty from the raids.

Ben McCulloch had been the first to cut the Comanche trail. He sounded the alarm, alerted Adam Zumwalt and John Tomlinson, who with a hundred and fifty men now dogged Buffalo Hump's rear guard on the retreat north. Ben, Jack and other San Antonio Rangers had ridden several horses almost to death spreading word of the raid. Now riders and messengers criss-crossed the rolling Texas landscape. Ranger companies converged on Plum Creek from Gonzales, Lavaca, Victoria, Cuero and other settlements.

From along the Colorado, Brazos and San Antonio rivers, merchants, farmers and frontiersmen loaded weapons and took to the saddle as word of the raid spread. They filtered into Plum Creek singly, in pairs, or in small groups. General Felix Huston had arrived at daybreak with a detachment of militia regulars, a few hours behind the eighty-seven-man force under Old Paint Caldwell. The veteran Texas Indian fighters deferred to Huston's rank; the general was now in command. A number of the Texans, Jack Hays included, were not pleased to have Huston in charge, but they trusted Caldwell and the other seasoned officers to point the general in the right direction when the time came.

Colonel Edward Burleson, with another eighty Texans and thirteen Tonkawa warriors, was now within an hour's march, moving at the gallop. The Tonkawas ran on foot alongside the Texans' horses, eager to battle their ancient Comanche enemies.

Buffalo Hump had made a serious tactical error.

Flushed with the success of the raid and hampered by the huge herd of stolen horses and pack mules, the Paneteka chief had chosen to return north by the same route he had taken on the drive south. *Greed and overconfidence will do in a Comanche the same as a white man,* Jack thought.

"I sure hope Huston pays attention to Old Paint and Colonel Burleson when the fiddler finishes tuning up," Bigfoot said. "What do you make the odds, Jack?"

"We're outnumbered about three to one, I'd guess."

Bigfoot Wallace chuckled aloud. "Well, damn me for a flat-tail 'possum. Looks like we got the edge for once."

Jack and Bigfoot made their way to Caldwell's side at the edge of the line of timber overlooking the Big Prairie of Plum Creek. Jack stood for a moment, again studying the battle site. Old Paint had chosen well. Now that he had committed himself, Buffalo Hump had to come this way, across Plum Creek to the Colorado, the only reliable source of water in times of drought. The stolen horses represented great riches to the Comanches. And horses needed water.

Brush and timber along Plum Creek concealed the waiting Texans. The raiders, coming up a shallow valley on the west side of the prairie, wouldn't see them until they were almost within rifle range. On the far side of the prairie stood a small grove of trees, the only cover available to the Indians. Jack had ridden out the grove and found there was little underbrush. A man could fight from horseback there.

To the north, a boggy seep fanned out for nearly a mile. It would slow the Indian retreat. The fight had to be here, and it had to end before the Indians reached the rugged Hill Country to the north. In the hills it would be all but impossible to close with the Indians in a decisive battle.

Jack studied Old Paint Caldwell's weathered face, now creased in a deep scowl. Jack knew the reason for the frown. General Felix Huston. Huston's plan was to attack the Indians from an open box formation. Caldwell's men under Ben McCulloch would have the left flank, Burleson's troops the right, and Major Monroe Hardeman's militia would close the rear of the box. Caldwell wanted more of an ambush, a quick cut. He wasn't going to get it. He had at least managed to convince Huston that the first objective of the Texans should be to stampede the Indian horse herd.

Huston's plan might work. But "might" was a big word in dealing with Comanches. The reality could be a pricklier sort of porcupine, Jack knew. *We're not likely to get any captives out alive,* he thought. *The best we can hope for is to hit the Comanches hard, make them kill the captives quickly.*

A scout came in at the gallop and slid his lathered mount to a stop. "They're coming, Colonel," he said to Caldwell, ignoring Huston. "About two miles back."

Old Paint nodded his thanks, then turned to Ben McCulloch. "Best get your men into position, Ben. The fandango's about to open. Jack, I'd like you and three others to stay with me in case we need a Ranger-style attack in this area." Caldwell turned to Huston. "General, I'd pass the word for the men to mount up."

Jack swung aboard his own mount. Judas seemed to sense the impending battle. Muscles quivered beneath Jack's knees. The horse snorted, shook his head and stamped his front feet nervously.

A billowing dust cloud and the flock of buzzards soaring above the lower end of the valley marked the approach of the Comanche column. The horse herd came into view first, a wide mass of brown and sorrel and buckskin and paint bodies moving diagonally from the mouth of the valley onto the wide dry-grass prairie. Half a hundred braves herded the stolen animals, whooping and yelling. Bright red and green calico streamers flowed from the manes and tails of the Indian mounts, spoils of the raid on Linnville.

"Hit 'em now, General," Jack heard Caldwell urge Huston. "We can spook the horses, stampede them back through the Indians."

"I don't know, Colonel. The captives—we'd have to divide our own forces—"

Jack clenched his own jaws in disgust at the militia general's indecision. The opportunity was lost while Huston tried to make up his mind.

Almost a half hour passed before the main body of Indians spilled onto the prairie, still unaware of the presence of the Texans in the brush.

Huston raised a hand and motioned the Texans forward. The mounted men rode from the brush at a slow walk, the militia infantry the last to march onto the plain.

A warrior yelped in surprise and pointed toward the Texans. The Indians milled in momentary confusion, shouting and cursing, then formed into a ragged battle line and moved cautiously toward the Texans. The distance between the two armies closed to less than three hundred yards.

Jack could now make out the dress and equipment of the Indians. Most wore white man's clothing plundered from Victoria and Linnville, but the tribal differences were still plain. It seemed to Jack that every tribe in Texas was represented. Paneteka, Wasp, Wanderer, even an occasional Kwahadi Comanche were there, along with Kiowa and Kiowa-Apache. Here and there rode an outlaw Wichita, Ute and Choctaw. Excited yelps and war whoops from the Indians split the heat and dust, a counterpoint to the near silence of the Texan line.

"First rank, advance and dismount. Fire when they're in range," Huston called.

A line of Texans moved fifty yards closer to the Indians, stepped from their saddles and raised rifles.

Six Indians broke from the Comanche lines, leaned low over their ponies' necks and charged into rifle range. The warriors fired arrows or hurled lances; all landed short of the Texan ranks. The riders then wheeled away untouched by rifle balls.

Jack ignored the displays of horsemanship by the Comanches. He watched as twenty Indians armed with rifles rode into the grove of trees across the plain. To his right another thirty or so warriors quirted ponies toward the Texans' right flank; the Comanche believed that if he could ride around an opposing force he was sure to defeat them. This group was in for a surprise, Jack thought. They were headed directly toward Burleson's sharp-shooters and the Tonkawas.

One impressive warrior chief, over six feet tall and wearing a stovepipe hat, took up the game and kneed his mount in a run toward the Texans. He wore a blue frock coat buttoned down the back, fine leather boots that climbed past his knees, and carried a white parasol. "Damned if he ain't pretty," Bigfoot Wallace muttered at Jack's side. The Indian spun his mount to the right, then the left, shouted taunts and curses toward the Texans and raced unharmed back into the Comanche ranks.

Gunshots began to crackle from the trees and were answered by Texas rifles, but little damage was done to either side. Jack glanced at the general in command. Huston seemed fascinated, frozen by the spectacle of Comanche horsemanship and daring.

"They're stalling, General." Caldwell's tone betrayed his exasperation. "They're just buying time to get the women and children away from the fight. They'll start killing captives any minute now. You've got to attack!"

Huston gave no sign that he had heard.

Jack heard the distinctive battle cries of the Tonkawas on the right flank, a rattle of gunshots and the startled yelps of Comanches. Moments later the warriors who had tried to turn the Texans' flank raced back into view. A half-dozen unmounted horses ran with them. *Bad sign for old Buffalo Hump,* Jack thought; *his braves couldn't get past the Tonks and ride around our boys. Now his warriors will be getting itchy about their chances.*

A tall, broad-shouldered Indian appeared at the front of the

Comanche ranks, sat in the saddle and stared toward the Texans in open contempt, his flowing headdress of feathers and beads spilling almost to the ground. It was the first time Jack had seen a full war bonnet among the Comanches. *Must be one mighty important chief,* he thought. The Indian kicked his horse into motion. A dozen Texas rifles cracked. The Comanche's body jerked, then sagged along his horse's neck. Two companions raced to his side, held him erect in the saddle and retreated to the safety of the Indian band. A long, high-pitched wail rose from the Indians. *More bad medicine,* Jack thought.

"Now, General!" Caldwell yelled. "Now is the time to charge them! They're whipped!"

Caldwell's cry seemed to jar Huston back to reality. He pulled his saber and swept it toward the Indian lines.

The Texas yell, as blood-curdling as any Comanche war whoop, erupted from the throats of Rangers as they spurred mounts into motion.

The Indians held their ground for a moment against the charge. First one, then another, crumpled to the ground or cried out in pain. The Indian line wavered, then steadied, encouraged by the rifle fire from the Comanches among the trees. The twenty warriors were not exceptional riflemen, but the mere presence of the long guns could blunt the Texans' attack and cost the lives of some good men.

Jack drove spurs into Judas. The sorrel was in a dead run within three strides, racing toward the trees. A ball whistled harmlessly past Jack's head. Another plucked at the sleeve of his shirt. He heard the pound of horses' hooves at his back and chanced a glance over his shoulder. Bigfoot Wallace, Bill Davis and Sam Walker were hot on Judas's heels. Then Jack was in the trees. He fired his rifle as Judas thundered past the Indians. The shot went wild. Jack slammed the rifle barrel against the neck of a warrior who was frantically pouring powder into the flashpan of an ancient flintlock musket.

The four Rangers ripped through the Indian riflemen, firing pistols, slashing with knives and swinging clubbed rifles, then spun their horses and charged again, kneeing their well-trained mounts through narrow openings between the trees. The resolve of the Indian riflemen broke under the assault. Warriors dropped their weapons and sprinted from the trees toward the safety of the larger Indian force.

The loss of the riflemen seemed to destroy what little fight was left in the Comanche raiding party. The Indians fell back before the now-constant rattle of Texas guns, then gave up the fight to ride for their lives.

The Battle of Plum Creek turned into a rout. The Indians split into small bands, pursued by groups of mounted Texans. Militia infantrymen stalked the few Comanches remaining on the prairie. By late afternoon the Texans had given up the chase and returned to the original battle site.

The scope of the fight took shape in Jack's mind, pieced from his own observations, reports that filtered in to Matthew Caldwell and bits of conversation. Scores of stolen horses and mules had hit the bog and mired. Texas riflemen picked off almost all the horse herders. Burleson and his men, led by the Tonkawas, chased one Comanche band almost to the banks of the San Marcos, leaving Indian dead and wounded in their wake. Other running battles stretched for miles before exhausted horses and the scattering of the Indians forced the Texans to end the pursuit.

Three captives had been recovered, including a woman whose whalebone corset had blunted the impact of an arrow. A physician had to yank at the arrow twice before finally wrenching it from her breast. She would live. Others weren't so fortunate. The Texans found bodies tied to trees and riddled with arrows and lance wounds. Among the dead was a granddaughter of Daniel Boone.

The Texas force recaptured most of the stolen horses and mules, and much of the plunder from Victoria and Linnville. They also had taken scores of Indian horses and hundreds of weapons. The loot that could be identified would be returned to the original owners. The rest was divided as spoils of war among the Texans and their Tonkawa allies. The Tonks who had arrived on foot would ride back home in style. They were now rich men.

As the day faded, Jack Hays squatted by a small fire alongside Bigfoot Wallace, Bill Davis and Old Paint Caldwell, sharing a supper of roasted mule meat, parched corn and stale biscuits from the colonel's saddlebags.

"Good day for Texas, considering," Caldwell said between bites. "We lost only one man and had seven wounded. Gave old Buffalo Hump one mighty big dose of bad medicine. Killed at least eighty Indians, probably more." Caldwell reached for another biscuit. "Jack, when you and the boys cleaned out that nest of rifles, it turned the whole shooting match around. Got rid of a threat and drove the Comanches right into our guns."

Bigfoot Wallace grinned and winked at Jack. "Yep. I reckon old Big Pisser here grew some in the view of them Comanch today. Man's got *cojones grandes,* that's for sure. Charge hell with a dipper of water and leave Old Scratch lookin' for a towel, he would."

Jack felt the heat rise in his cheeks at the unwanted praise.

Bill Davis wiped a sleeve across greasy lips. "Colonel Caldwell, any chance this will end our Comanche troubles?"

Caldwell grimaced. "No, son. We won the battle, but we're a damn fine distance from winning the war. We might slow 'em down some. Comanches lost a lot of war medicine here, but they aren't whipped, not by a damn sight. The colonel ran a hand through gray-streaked hair. "Only way to get rid of the Comanches is to push them clear to hell out of Texas. And that is going to take some heavy doing."

An hour later Jack sat alone by the fading embers of the camp fire, listening to the Tonkawa victory celebration nearby. The Tonks had roasted and eaten a few choice morsels carved from the Comanche bodies. White men who didn't know the Tonks might find the idea of cannibalism repugnant, but it made sense to the Tonkawa. Consume part of your beaten enemy and you add his strength to your own.

The Tonks had earned the right.

Now it was time to go home.

FIVE

San Antonio
September 1840

Jack Hays carefully refolded the document bearing the official seal of the Republic of Texas and tucked it into a desk drawer. President Mirabeau B. Lamar had handed him a mountain lion with a sore tooth and asked him to carry it by the tail.

John Coffee Hays was now a Texas Ranger captain with the job of expanding the San Antonio Ranger detachment. That sounded simple enough on the surface. There were plenty of good men to draw from as a cadre of seasoned fighters and no small supply of citizens who were willing, even eager, to join the company. Jack had no more than thirty men under his command. Lamar wanted him to triple the size of the detachment to a hundred Rangers.

The biggest fly in this jar of syrup was Lamar's order to "safeguard the region from the Indian menace and resist invasion by Mexican troops." Jack wished it was as simple as Lamar made it sound.

San Antonio was still the western frontier of Texas. Plum Creek hadn't changed the fact that a few miles from the edge of the city to the west and north was Comanche country. To the south were the Mexicans and San Antonio was the prize that set every would-be hero following the Snake-and-Eagle flag to salivating.

Outside the small stone building a mockingbird trilled its way through an endless variation of song in the warm, still air of a lingering summer. Jack sensed it would be a long time until first frost, even longer until the howl of the north wind chased the Comanches into winter quarters. Until then it would be one skirmish after another, one dead Texan after another. And the constant patrols from the Nueces to the Hill Country. Jack glanced through the window at the bird perched in a cottonwood tree. "You wouldn't be so happy about it if you were wearing our tailfeathers," he muttered to the mockingbird. White bands flashed on wings and tail as the bird fluttered to another tree without missing a note in flight. *How can they do that,* Jack wondered; *seems like it would be awfully hard to fly and sing at the same time.*

Jack's letter of commission from President Lamar hadn't impressed the local merchants and blacksmiths a great deal. The scrip and warrants of the Republic of Texas were losing value by the day. Soon they would be worth little more than paper for the outhouse. Jack already was out two hundred dollars of his own hard currency for horseshoes and other necessities of his Ranger company. He didn't begrudge the personal expense. A gold piece here and there might mean the difference between the Republic's survival or death.

"Captain Hays?"

Jack turned toward the door. A slender youth stood in the doorway, a dispatch pouch slung over a shoulder.

"Yes?"

"Letter for you, sir." The youth pulled an envelope from the pouch and handed it to Jack. "Colonel Karnes felt it too important to trust to normal mail channels. I'm Thad Green, the colonel's personal dispatch rider."

Jack extended a hand. The boy's grip was firm, the palm and fingers callused. The calluses told Jack that Thad Green was no stranger to horses and lariat ropes. "Pleased to meet you, Thad. Something to drink?"

Thad Green licked parched lips. "If you can spare some cool water, sir. It's been a dry trail out."

"There's a fresh pail and a dipper on the table here. Drink your fill, then have a seat."

Thad declined the offered chair. "If you don't mind, sir, I'll stand. I've been a while in the saddle."

Jack nodded. He slipped his knife from its sheath and opened the letter. He almost didn't recognize Henry Karnes's handwriting. The script was shaky. The words almost ran together, and the lines slanted downward across the page. Jack looked up at Thad Green in growing concern. "Is Colonel Karnes feeling worse, Thad?"

Moisture glistened at the corner of the youth's eyes. "Not any longer, sir. Colonel Karnes died two days ago. The letter you're holding was the last thing he wrote, just a few hours before he passed on."

The heaviness of loss settled in Jack's gut. The red-haired Karnes had been more than just a commanding officer to Jack. He was a friend. "I'm sorry, Thad, truly sorry," Jack said. He had to push the words through the tightness in his throat. "Colonel Karnes was a good man."

"Yes, sir, he was. He was like a father to me." Thad Green squared his shoulders, trying not to show his grief. "I didn't stay for the funeral. I thought I could serve his memory better by hurrying this message along."

Jack nodded and turned his attention back to the dispatch:

Dear Jack:

Please excuse the brevity and informality of this letter. I have learned of something that brought to mind our conversation after the Verde Creek fight with the Comanches.

A young man named Samuel Colt has invented a repeating revolver, developed for the U.S. Navy. The Navy, short-sighted as usual, can't see the value of the weapon. I think you will see it immediately. The gun shoots *five times* without reloading!

A gross of these guns, called the Paterson Colt, are now in the Navy storehouse at Washington-on-the-Brazos. If you are able to obtain the guns, they might be the tool to give our Rangers an advantage over our enemies.

In closing, if you need another good man, I can recommend young Thad Green, bearer of this letter. He has

Ranger qualities and needs only your guidance and training. He is eager to join your group.

I am glad to have called you friend, Jack.

The letter was signed simply,

HENRY W. KARNES

Jack's fingers trembled as he refolded the dispatch and slipped it into its envelope. A growing sense of excitement took the edge from his hurt over Henry Karnes's death. *A weapon like that would make one Ranger the equal of five men,* he thought, *and we could fight from horseback.* He glanced at Thad Green. "The colonel says you want to be a Texas Ranger, Thad. His recommendation is more than enough for me. Are you up to riding to Washington-on-the-Brazos?"

"Yes, sir."

"Then I'll give you the oath of office on the way, Ranger Green," Jack said. "Let me grab my saddlebags and a couple of friends named Wallace and Walker. We're going to borrow some Navy guns."

Washington-on-the-Brazos
September 1840

The naval officer on duty at the supply depot frowned and shook his head at the four men standing before him.

"Captain Hays, I'm sorry. I can't release weapons from Navy stores to civilians—even Texas Rangers—without specific authorization from my commanding officer."

Jack Hays forced a smile through embers of anger. "Even though the Army and Navy have no use for them?"

"Sorry, Captain. Those are my orders."

Jack sighed. "I understand, Lieutenant, and I commend you for your vigilance and dedication to orders." Jack glanced at Bigfoot Wallace and Sam Walker. The Rangers' scowls mirrored his own feelings. He knew Wallace and Walker, given free rein, would simply club the officer and take the Colts; even young

Thad Green had his teeth clenched and looked as if he might give Bigfoot and Sam a hand. Jack caught Walker's eye and shook his head in warning. They couldn't help the Rangers if they were all in a Navy brig.

"Well, Lieutenant," Jack said, "aside from arms, can you release other supplies for frontier defense? Things like wagon parts, blankets or maybe warm pea jackets? With proper authorization, of course."

The lieutenant smiled and nodded, obviously relieved that the Rangers weren't going to press the issue and perhaps cause trouble. "Yes, sir. I can issue such items on an interservice arrangement. With authorization, as you say. From a commissioned officer in a branch of a regular service of the Texas military." The officer swallowed. "Meaning no disrespect to your own rank or organization, Captain," he added lamely.

"Would a requisition from a Texas militia colonel suffice for such items?"

"Yes, sir." The young officer was now eager to oblige.

"Very well. May we inspect your stores, Lieutenant? I would hate to embarrass myself by making the wrong requests, and perhaps wind up with thirty yards of hawser and a brace of sails instead of the items we need."

"Certainly, sir. If you'll follow me?"

Jack waved away the suggestion with a reassuring smile. "You needn't bother, Lieutenant. You should remain on your post here. After all, there *are* thieves about. My friends and I can locate the equipment we need."

"Very well, sir. If you have any problems finding something, just let me know."

Jack nodded his thanks, turned to walk into the dim light of the storehouse interior, then paused. "By the way, Lieutenant," he said casually, "if you have one of those requisition forms on hand, it would save us all some time. We'll just jot down what we need as we check your stores."

"Yes, sir." The lieutenant reached into a desk drawer, produced a blank form and a stub of a pencil.

They were well out of earshot of the young officer when Bigfoot muttered, "What the hell are you up to, Jack?"

"Simple," Jack said. "They won't give us the pistols. We handle the problem the next best way. We steal them."

The sun had set when the Rangers returned to the Navy depot. Thad Green waited outside in a sturdy wagon. The lieutenant had gone off duty, as Jack had calculated, leaving an enlisted man in charge. The sailor didn't question the signature on the requisition. Jack knew Old Paint Caldwell wouldn't mind the forgery, and he was a militia colonel. As far as the Navy was concerned, all the papers were in order.

Jack waved away the sailor's offer to help load. "We'll take care of it ourselves," Jack said. "We know where everything is. My thanks to the Navy. With winter coming on, the Rangers need all the gum coats and blankets we can get."

Thirty minutes later Sam Walker grunted aloud as he heaved the last wooden box into the wagon bed. "Heaviest damn blankets I ever saw," Sam said with a grin and a wink.

Jack led the way as the party headed for the edge of town and the road to San Antonio.

"Jack," Bigfoot said, "that was one slick bit of card-sharpin'. Remind me not to ever get in a faro game with you."

Jack's chuckle was soft in the growing darkness. "We got what we came for, Bigfoot. Now let's put some distance between us and the Navy before anybody finds out what we've *really* got here."

They rode in silence until the full moon rose fat and red in the eastern sky. Within the hour its light would be bright enough to read a letter by. Jack called a halt to rest the wagon team. "Gentlemen," he said, "it occurs to me that someone is going to have to train the rest of our men to use these weapons. At first light, let's break out a couple each and get acquainted with them."

San Antonio
October 1840

Jack Hays watched in satisfaction as his company of Rangers went through a complex pattern of maneuvers on the plain outside

San Antonio, firing the new Paterson revolvers on the run from horseback, first with the right hand, then the left. Most adept of all with the weapon was young Thad Green, an expert horseman who could control his mount with his knees and shift his weight while firing with both hands—and still score hits on six of ten shots.

Jack admitted to a touch of awe at young Green's ability. Jack had never claimed to be a crack shot himself. Adequate, but not in the mold of Sam Walker, Ben McCulloch or Bigfoot Wallace, and to see Green handle a pistol so well and with such natural talent was a matter of wonder.

The Paterson Colt had some drawbacks, Jack conceded. The thirty-four-caliber ball lacked the wallop of the big horse pistols. It was barrel-heavy with an awkward grip which bulged at the base. The straight trigger disappeared into the frame until the gun was cocked, when it dropped down for use. There was no trigger guard; a man had to be careful when handling a cocked Paterson or risk putting a ball through his own thigh—or something a hell of a lot worse if he happened to be carrying the pistol stuck into the waistband of his pants at the time.

The biggest flaw in the weapon, to Jack's thinking, was in reloading. To recharge or change cylinders, the shooter had to depress a snap lock on the side of the barrel housing and remove the barrel, which dropped the cylinder free of the receiver and grip assembly. Reloading while handling three separate pieces of pistol and controlling a horse was the devil's own job for a man with just two hands.

But if the Paterson did have some flaws, the Rangers loved it anyway, like a good woman who happened to be a little ugly. Most important was the fact that the Colt put five shots in their hand without reloading. The extra four shots made up for the pistol's shortcomings. For the first time, Texas Rangers could fight from horseback like Indians or Mexican lancers.

Ben McCulloch reined his mount to a stop beside Jack. A broad grin creased Ben's normally expressionless face. "By God, Jack," he said, "I believe some Indians and Mexicans are in for a surprise now. For the first time, I'm kind of looking forward to a good fight."

"You may not have long to wait, Ben. One of our Lipan scouts rode in ten minutes ago. There's a Comanche raiding party headed south down the Nueces. Tell the men to saddle fresh horses. We ride in twenty minutes.''

Jack Hays studied the horizon above Nueces Canyon. A flock of big birds smeared the chill blue sky. Jack glanced at the tall, broad-shouldered Ranger at his side. ''Here's where you get your fight, Ben.''

Ben stared toward the canyon. ''Lot of buzzards up there. That means lots of Indians.'' He patted the two revolvers thrust into his waistband. ''But, what the hell. There's nineteen of us, all with Sam Colt as a saddle partner.''

Thad Green kneed his mount alongside the two veteran frontiersmen. The youth's face was pale, but his jaw was firm and eyes bright with anticipation. ''They know we're here, Captain,'' he said to Jack. ''I saw one of the Indians on top of the far ridge. He went riding hell for leather back toward the camp.''

Jack nodded. ''I saw him too, Thad. No chance for an ambush this time.'' He turned in the saddle to face the other Rangers. ''Let's go, men. You all know what to do.''

The Rangers rode leisurely up the broad, flat bottom of Nueces Canyon, giving no outward sign they knew of the Indian presence. They were three hundred yards from the Comanche camp when the first group of warriors, about thirty strong, charged onto the plain. Jack estimated the Indians' total fighting strength at about seventy.

At Jack's signal the Rangers dismounted, rifles at the ready. The Indians, whooping in jubilation at catching a Texan force in the open, quirted their mounts into a dead run. At a hundred and fifty yards, twenty rifles cracked. Four Indians were knocked from ponies or went down with their wounded mounts.

The main body of Comanches spilled into the charge. Jack knew what they were thinking. The Texans had no rifles in reserve, caught in the open with no place to take cover or fort up. It would be the biggest Comanche victory since Linnville.

''Mount up!'' Jack called. Rangers sheathed rifles and pulled pistols as they mounted. The Indians were almost upon them. ''Charge! Powder-burn them!''

The Texan war cry roared from nineteen throats as the Rangers drove home the spurs. The Indians checked their mounts in reflex, some forgetting to loose their arrows in the shock and surprise at the unexpected Texan charge.

The Rangers tore into and through the front rank of Comanches, smoke and lead belching from handguns. Jack saw the disbelief on one warrior's face before a ball from Jack's pistol ripped into the Indian's forehead. He thumbed the Paterson, fired at a second Comanche. The shot went wild, but a third ball thumped home.

The warriors yelped in confusion, too stunned to fight back. The Rangers rode so close among them that the Comanche bows were useless. Texans fired point-blank into Indian bodies. Powder smoke and dust swirled thick over Nueces Canyon. The Comanches panicked. Bows, lances and shields fell to the earth, discarded as warriors bent low over their horses' necks. All pretense of fight abandoned, they rode for their lives. The Texans were wild men, riding instead of running, shooting as though each finger of their hands had become the barrel of a gun. Such medicine was as frightening as it was strong. Not even the bravest warrior could stand against such power. From the corner of his eye, Jack saw Thad Green empty his pistol, leaving two Indians down in his wake, then draw a second gun from his belt. Ben's deep-throated, distinctive battle yell pierced the clamor of startled and wounded Indians and the steady bark of the Paterson pistols. The running battle covered three miles before Jack pulled his horse to a stop. He lifted the big horse pistol from its saddle holster and fired the signal to break off the attack. There was no mistaking the deep cough of the heavy-bore pistol against the lighter, spiteful crack of the Patersons.

An eerie calm settled over the trail of Indian bodies in the canyon, broken only by an occasional gunshot as a Ranger finished off a wounded Comanche. Jack's orders were specific. Take no prisoners. This was a punitive strike, one to carry a message to all the Texas Plains tribes: The Texas Rangers now had new and powerful medicine.

As Jack rode through the trail of bodies, he knew the frontier wars had taken an abrupt turn. The Paterson made the difference. *The war's just gone horseback,* Jack thought, *and, by God, we may even have a chance to win now.* He paused to reload both his pistols, charge his rifle and count his casualties.

Not a single Texan had been lost.

Ben McCulloch had a minor wound across his thigh, a lance cut which barely broke the skin. The blood was already beginning to clot. Thad Green had lost a piece of his left earlobe. The youth grinned as he dabbed at the nick. Bill Davis sucked at a gash across his knuckles. The only serious Ranger injury had come not at the hands of the Indians, but when Ed Begley's horse stepped in a badger hole, fell and broke the rider's arm. The horse limped from a slight muscle sprain but would recover. Jack was relieved at that. The worst duty a Ranger could draw was to have to shoot a good horse.

Jack counted thirty-two dead Comanches in the canyon. Buzzards already were floating down, landing ponderously to tear at the bodies.

At the site where the fight began, Ben McCulloch fired the final shot of the Nueces Canyon battle. His rifle ball dispatched a wounded Comanche who had climbed partway up the canyon wall.

As the echoes of the rifle shot died away, Bill Davis reached for his canteen and raised the container above his head. "Men, let's drink to the newest member of the Texas Rangers—Colonel Sam Colt!"

Jack joined the toast, then handed his canteen to the Ranger with the broken arm. Ed Begley drank, then winced as Jack pulled the fractured bones back into alignment and splinted the break with sticks and thick leather carved from the skirt of a captured Indian saddle. Begley chuckled through the pain as Jack tied down the splint.

"Old Bigfoot and Sam Walker are gonna be mad they missed the fun," Begley said.

"I expect you're right, Ed," Jack said, "but somebody has to fish for Mexicans. We don't want them swimming in Texas rivers." He pulled the final knot tight. "Break was clean. It should heal all right. I have a pint in a saddlebag. You need a slug to ease the pain?"

"Nah. Save it in case somebody really gets hurt. I still got one good arm for shootin' if need be, and whiskey throws my aim off some. I'll get me a drink come Christmas and New Year's."

SIX

Austin
New Year's Eve 1840

The new capital of the Republic of Texas was little more than a cluster of buildings atop a bluff, but it was already taking on an air of permanence, Jack Hays noted as he strode along the rough split logs of the sidewalk along the town's main street.

Streamers and banners of red and green, now showing the wear of weather, fluttered from windows and over doorways in celebration of the season. A sharp north wind howled against the back of the new stone building which Jack understood would soon become the Republic's Hall of State.

Jack paused outside the doorway. The music from inside was of surprisingly professional quality. He wondered why he had been invited—ordered might be a better word—to this particular event in the fledgling town.

Austin sat on the edge of the frontier, hard against Comanche country, seventy miles from San Antonio. To Jack it seemed the location was less than ideal for a seat of government. He wondered if the optimism of Lamar and the Austin backers were mere dreams, or if one day the city would, in fact, be the central point of a bustling nation sprawling from the Sabine to the Red River to the vast dry plains of the Llano Estacado and even beyond. Perhaps Shakespeare's line from *The Tempest*, "We are such stuff as dreams are made on," might apply, Jack thought, but it's rather unlikely old Will had Texans in mind when he penned that bit of wisdom.

He wiped the soles of his boots across a coarse woven mat at the door and stepped inside the hall. A hardwood floor, a rarity on the frontier, spanned the entire length of the room. Along one wall tables sagged under mounds of food and drink. Roaring fireplaces at either end of the hall and the heat from a dozen oil lamps held the winter chill at bay with a little too much ferocity for Jack's taste. The room was crowded with dancers, the women in layers of holiday finery as they spun across the dance floor in the arms of men in swallowtail coats and vests.

Jack felt more than a little out of place in his simple black suit and string tie. The collar of the boiled white shirt chafed his neck. He would rather have been in San Antonio. There, Mary Maverick, perpetually smiling and almost as perpetually pregnant, would be hosting a less lavish but more satisfying party. At Mary's, formality was less important than comradeship. Across town from the Mavericks' home, Antonio Perez, one of the Mexican Texans whose loyalty to the Republic was beyond question, would be presiding over a *baile* of monumental proportions. Jack knew that many of his Rangers—at least those who were not on duty—would feel the effects of the hospitality of Perez and the Mavericks tomorrow morning.

Jack recognized a few of the faces in the crowded ballroom. Some had traveled all the way from East Texas, others from communities along the Gulf Coast. This was obviously the social event of the year in Texas.

"Jack! Captain Jack Hays!" The familiar voice of Colonel Matthew Caldwell boomed across the crowded hall.

Old Paint weaved his way through the dancers to grab Jack's hand. "Damn, Jack, but it's good to see you again. Haven't had a chance to tell you what a hell of a job you did on the Indians in Nueces Canyon. God, what a fight! The whole of Texas is talking about it."

"I didn't do much of anything, Colonel," Jack said. "It was the Colt pistol that made the difference. That and the men I ride with."

"No matter. You and your boys are legends on the frontier already. And you haven't hurt young Sam Colt's reputation any, either. Everybody's calling that pistol of his the 'Texas Model,' and everybody wants one all of a sudden.'' The colonel clapped the smaller man on the shoulder. ''Come along. There's some people who want to meet you. I didn't ask you to ride all the way to Austin in a blue whistler just to fandango. Speaking of which, how about a drink to cut the chill?''

Jack shook his head. ''Later, maybe. One for the new year.''

Caldwell raised his gaze skyward in mock prayer. ''God, how can I trust a man who doesn't smoke, drink or gamble? We Texans have a reputation to uphold. Now I've got to take care of this man's end of the jug too, and I'll pay for it in the morning.''

Caldwell steered Jack toward a room at the back of the hall and shoved the door open. A dozen men were crowded into the room, some seated around a rough wood table, others in chairs along the walls, all in formal attire. Most had the pale, washed-out look of men who spent most of their time indoors. A few of them looked like they could still fork a horse and pull a trigger, Jack thought. Cigar and pipe smoke layered the upper third of the small room. The ceiling was all but invisible through the blue-gray haze. Jack's eyes stung. He didn't object to pipes, but the cigars laid a heavy stink in his nostrils, more acrid than the scent of black powder. *This group wouldn't be worth a sore-backed horse on patrol,* Jack thought; *any sober Comanche could smell them a mile off.*

''Jack, I'd like you to meet David G. Burnett, current vice president of the Republic,'' Caldwell said, ''and if the voters have the sense God gave a rock, soon to open a second time around as president.''

A stocky man with graying hair and a noticeable paunch rose and offered a hand to Jack. ''It is a pleasure to meet you, Captain Hays,'' Burnett said. ''The President has asked me to express his personal regards and his appreciation for what you have accomplished on our frontier. And his regrets that he cannot be here in person to convey his feelings. May I present a few of President Lamar's associates?''

Jack Hays soon realized he was in the company of men who held the future of the Republic in hand. Among the group were

Abner S. Lipscomb, secretary of state; F. A. Morris, attorney general; James W. Simmons, treasurer; and a half-dozen others with close personal or political ties to the Lamar administration.

It was Burnett who answered Jack's unasked question.

"We've asked you here, Captain Hays, for a couple of reasons. First of all, the President has asked me to sound you out on the possibility of joining the administration. I've been authorized to offer you a key post in the government."

Jack did not hesitate in his reply. "With all due respect, sir, I must decline. I'm not a politician. I'm a Texas Ranger, and that's all I want to be at the moment. Please inform the President I am flattered at his interest."

Matthew Caldwell chuckled aloud and held out a hand, palm up, to Lipscomb. "Told you so, Abner."

Lipscomb pulled a silver dollar from his pocket and dropped it into Caldwell's hand. "It's worth a dollar to finally meet somebody who *doesn't* want to be a politician," the secretary of state said with a wry smile.

"Very well, Captain. We respect your openness. And your decision," Burnett said. "Now, let's get down to some serious business." Burnett pulled a fresh cigar from his pocket, nipped off the end of the cylinder and spat the sliver of tobacco into the fireplace. He twirled the cigar between his palms for a moment before lighting it over the flame of an oil lamp. No one else in the room spoke. Apparently, Jack decided, this was Burnett's show.

The vice president turned to Jack. "Captain Hays, there are developments afoot that you should know about. These developments will have a momentous impact on your Ranger company. Probably a dangerous impact." Burnett began to pace as best he could in the confined quarters. "President Lamar may be a dreamer in some ways, Captain, but he is more of a realist than most people realize. Or care to admit. He recognizes, as do I, that Sam Houston probably will be elected president of the Republic—despite Colonel Caldwell's optimism. As Houston's opponent it pains me to admit it, but he holds the whip hand. It's becoming increasingly clear that I'm going to lose the election. But not without a fight, mind you."

Burnett worried the cigar, trailing a blue cloud as he walked.

"I'm sure you are aware that Houston and President Lamar are almost exact opposites in their view of the future of Texas. Houston's election, barring an unseen miracle, would probably undo all that President Lamar has gained." Burnett stopped pacing before Jack. "Captain Hays, what is your estimate of the current status of the frontier in general and San Antonio in particular, regarding the Indian and Mexican threat?"

Jack paused, unconsciously running a thumb along his jaw as he considered the question. "Mister Burnett, we've somewhat blunted the danger from the Comanches, at least as far as large raiding parties are concerned. They were badly mauled at Plum Creek and in Colonel John Moore's raid on the Red Fork of the Colorado deep in Comancheria last October. But the Comanches are far from being whipped, sir. We'll have our hands full with them for years to come."

"And the Mexicans?"

"We have reports that more troops are moving into northern Mexico. I don't like the sound of it."

"Captain Hays, I don't have to remind you that San Antonio is the key to the Republic. It's our westernmost fort on the frontier. If the Mexicans invade, can you hold?"

"Realistically, no. We don't have the men or resources to stop a major Mexican offensive. I have less than seventy Rangers in my company, with perhaps a couple hundred more volunteers who would respond to the call. The best we could do would be a holding action. Maybe, with luck, we could keep an army at bay for a few days until more help arrived. To tell you otherwise would be a lie, pure and simple."

"I understand, Captain," Burnett said.

Jack smiled. "On the other hand, sir, reality never stopped a Texan. Tell him he can't do something and he'll bust his butt to prove you wrong."

Burnett exhaled a cloud of blue-gray cigar smoke. "That's what we're counting on, Captain Hays. God, as Voltaire wrote, is on the side not of the heavy battalions, but of the best shots."

"If I may be so bold, Mister Vice President, there is another famous quotation which might apply here as well," Jack said. " 'So was the huntsman by the bear oppress'd, Whose hide he sold—before he caught the beast.' "

Burnett chuckled. "Apt point, Captain. And I must admit I never expected to meet another man who knew the writings of Edmund Waller." The vice president's expression faded into a frown. He plucked the cigar from his lips and rolled it in his fingers. "What I'm about to tell you, Captain Hays, is not to leave this room. President Lamar is about to set in motion several plans that will force the United States to annex Texas. On *our* terms. It also probably will place the men under your command in jeopardy."

Burnett resumed his pacing. "President Lamar," he said brusquely, "hopes to push Mexico into war."

Jack felt a sudden tightness clamp about his chest; his breath caught momentarily in his throat.

"The President," Burnett continued, "has decided to send an expedition to Santa Fe to take command of the Mexican capital there. He believes, and I concur, that the residents of New Mexico will mount an insurrection and cast their lot with Texas." Burnett paused before a table against a wall, poured a small measure of whiskey into a drinking glass and sipped at the liquid.

"At this moment," he said solemnly, "the President is preparing a declaration claiming the new boundary of the Republic of Texas as the Rio Grande. And a declaration that Texas is laying claim to the Californias on the West Coast." Burnett lifted the whiskey glass as if to propose a toast. "Gentlemen," Burnett said, "the Republic of Texas is about to spread to another sea. By the time Houston takes office, so many wheels will be rolling that he simply won't be able to stop the chariot."

A momentary silence settled over the gathering. Jack forced himself to push aside his own doubts, to reach for the logic behind Lamar's bold moves. Burnett was right in some respects. Houston's Peace Party couldn't turn back what had already happened. The United States could not afford to have a strong Texas with powerful European allies at its back door, blocking any future westward expansion. And when the Union annexed Texas, American forces would have to be thrown into any war with Mexico. *In the meantime, we're cannon fodder,* he thought.

"Now, gentlemen," Burnett said, "let's put politics aside and welcome in the year 1841. Perhaps it will be a vintage year. Let's join the party."

Jack followed Old Paint Caldwell from the stuffy, smoky room into the less oppressive air of the main hall.

"Well, Jack," Caldwell said with a heavy sigh, "it looks like we've been handed a dozen mad rattlers and a sack with a hole in the bottom to put 'em in. At least we can have some fun before the horse apples hit us. We worry *mañana, a la Mexicano.* Meantime, come along. There's someone I want you to meet. Someone who's *not* trying to get us all spitted on a Mexican lance."

Caldwell led Jack across the room to a cluster of young men gathered beside a half-empty punch bowl. He shouldered his way through the crowd to the chair where a lone girl sat.

"Miss Susan Calvert, may I present Captain John Coffee Hays of the Texas Rangers. Jack Hays, Susan Calvert."

Jack tried not to stare and failed. Susan Calvert's oval face was framed by dark brown hair burnished in auburn highlights. Soft, wide-set and intelligent brown eyes stared back above a straight, slightly freckled nose and full lips raised in a smile that dug deep dimples into otherwise smooth cheeks. The pale green gown she wore hugged the slender figure beneath. She was, Jack realized, the most beautiful woman he'd ever seen.

"I'm so pleased to meet you, Captain Hays." Susan Calvert's voice was like the husky rustle of a spring-fed stream swirling past polished stones. "I've heard so much about you." She extended a hand. Jack took it, aware of the warmth and subtle strength of the slender fingers as he bowed above her hand.

"The pleasure is mine, Miss Calvert." Jack found himself groping in vain for something else to say.

Susan Calvert made no effort to withdraw her hand until Jack slowly became aware he had been holding it for an unusually long time. He finally released his grip and felt the color rise in his cheeks. He knew he was good at handling horses and men. He also knew he was out of his element around a woman of quality and quiet elegance. This was no ordinary señorita to be danced, tequilaed and forgotten before sunrise.

"Colonel Caldwell has told me of some of your exploits, Captain Hays."

"Don't worry, Jack," Old Paint said with a wink, "I only told her the socially acceptable parts."

Susan laughed, a throaty chuckle that started in the middle of a musical scale and slid downward. It seemed to suit her, Jack thought. He glanced around, aware for the first time of the bleak stares of jealousy from the other young men gathered around Susan Calvert. He realized he was in enemy territory. The knowledge seemed to relax Jack, as though he were surrounded by Comanches and gearing for a fight. He welcomed the familiar calm. It let him cast aside the curtain of awe that had him momentarily tongue-tied. He smiled at Susan, ignoring the men.

"Miss Calvert, you really shouldn't believe everything Colonel Caldwell tells you," Jack said. "He's a fine soldier and a good friend, but I wouldn't want him as a character witness."

Old Paint Caldwell guffawed. "You've got that right, Jack Hays. Excuse me—I have to go see a friend, one I have not yet met, about liberating a tumbler of good Kentucky bourbon from yonder bar."

Jack smiled at Susan. "Might I be so bold as to ask you to dance, Miss Calvert? I must warn you, however, that I'm not especially good at it."

She offered her arm. He led her onto the dance floor, letting her scent of lilac wash the sting of cigar smoke from his nostrils. She turned into his arms. Jack tried to concentrate on executing the technique of the waltz instead of the heady feel of the woman. After a few steps he was able to relax and let the music take over his muscles. The dance ended too soon for Jack.

"Captain Hays," Susan said as he escorted her back toward her seat, "my father and I are thinking of moving to western Texas. It seems like fertile ground for horse raising, and one of our major interests is the breeding of good stock from Kentucky lineage. We've been looking at a small ranch near Seguin. Do you think it would be safe there?"

Jack hesitated. He wanted to warn her that the whole of the Texas frontier was about to be whipped into one big prairie fire. But he had pledged his silence. "Miss Calvert, I'd be less than honest if I told you yes. No place in Texas west of the Trinidad River is safe, and won't be until the Indians have been removed and the danger of invasion by Mexico has passed." Jack helped her into a straight-backed chair, reluctant to release his light grip on her arm. "I suppose Seguin is about as safe as any place out here, if your father is determined to settle. There are good men there, Rangers and volunteers, to provide protection. Personally, I would much prefer that you not take the risk at this time."

"Thank you for your honesty, Captain Hays." Susan's dark eyes reflected the lamplight as she gazed into his face. "I appreciate your concern."

Reluctantly, Jack bowed to take his leave when the band struck up a bright tune.

"Captain Hays?"

"Yes?"

"Would you think it terribly forward of me to suggest that you ask me to dance again?"

He reached for her hand.

Laredo
February 1841

Captain Jack Hays let his hand drift to the pistol thrust into his waistband. The grip of the Paterson Colt was reassuring to the touch, especially when a man was about to ride into the middle of a detachment of Mexican soldiers on their home grounds. President Lamar could declare and proclaim until a crow sang like a mockingbird, but Laredo was still in Mexico.

The dusty, sun-baked cluster of adobe and stucco huts on the upward bend of the Rio Grande had become an important link in the chain of supplies which flowed in increasing volume from merchants in northern Mexico to the stores and warehouses of San Antonio.

Mexicans, Jack thought, were like most businessmen. National pride was one thing. Profit was another. With the scarcity of hard currency on the frontier, barter was essential to the survival of San Antonio and to the Mexican merchants alike. Mexican traders brought beans, flour, sugar, leather, shoes, saddles and other basic goods to the city to trade for calico, tobacco and hardware items that were scarce in Mexico but plentiful in Texas. Both sides gained from the arrangement. The Mexican supply line had become as important to San Antonio as the freight wagons from East Texas and the distant seaports of the coast.

As the trade increased, so did the number of Mexican troops moving into the arid region known as the Mustang Desert between the Rio Grande and the Nueces. The number of bandits preying on the trade routes had grown faster than the troops. Either the Army or the bandits could seriously hamper trade or even cut the supply lines completely. Part of Jack's job was to blunt that threat.

Jack waved his fourteen-man patrol to a halt three miles from Laredo as Thad Green cantered back toward the group. The young man had learned well. He had become almost as good a scout and spy as Bigfoot or Sam Walker. Jack had no qualms about sending him on important missions.

"They're there, Captain Jack," Green said. "Thirty, forty infantry, another twenty dragoons and lancers. The saddle horses and pack animals are in a corral on the southwest side of the central plaza."

"The commander?"

"Only saw one officer, a major."

Jack turned in the saddle. "All right, men. You know what to do. Make sure the Mexicans see your guns, but don't draw them unless they decide they want to fight. We're here to deliver a message, not kill Mexicans."

Bigfoot Wallace snorted in disgust.

"Be patient, Bigfoot," Jack cautioned. "You'll get all the Mexicans you want, but not this time." Jack reined his horse toward Laredo.

The Ranger patrol moved into the town at a steady walk, Jack Hays in the lead. The Rangers looked neither right nor left as they moved into the heart of the Mexican encampment. Bewildered Mexican troops stood and stared as the Rangers rode past; they were unwilling to challenge the scowling, heavily armed Texans who had appeared as if from the parched soil itself.

The Mexican major stepped from a building, hand on his sword. He looked as if he might shout an order to the stunned soldiers. Jack fixed a steady, hard gaze on the officer's face in an unspoken warning. The major remained silent.

Bigfoot Wallace dismounted at the pole corral as the Rangers moved into position along the fence. Bigfoot slid the poles aside. Sam Walker rode into the corral, cut out a dozen Mexican horses and herded them through the gate. Jack took the point, the loose horses obediently falling into step behind Jack's sorrel. Other Rangers moved into place around the *remuda*.

The silence was broken only by the occasional snort of a horse or creak of saddle leather. Not a word was spoken by either side as the Rangers herded the horses from Laredo.

Jack called a halt in a shallow valley flanked by low, rocky hills two miles from town, posted lookouts on the hilltops, set a line of sentinels on his perimeter and put two men in charge of the horse herd.

"What now, Captain Jack?"

Jack looked up from the small fire he had started. "We wait, Thad. Tomorrow morning, we take the horses back."

Jack relieved Sam Walker at midnight, taking his turn at standing watch on the hilltop nearest Laredo. There was no sign of movement across the moon-washed prairie below. In the distance a coyote yipped twice and howled; a night hawk swooped to the ground nearby, then flapped aloft with effort, a rodent of some type squealing in the bird's talons. Jack glanced toward the north star. For an instant he thought his nostrils picked up a faint scent of lilac water. *Where is she tonight,* he wondered silently. Then he forced the thought of Susan Calvert from his mind.

The sun was halfway up the sky, a flat yellow disk flirting with wispy high clouds, as the Rangers herded the horses back into Laredo. Jack pulled Judas to a stop before the Mexican major. He sat for a moment and glared at the officer. "Major," Jack said in Spanish, "consider this a warning. There will be no other. If your command crosses into Texas, you and your people will be shot."

Jack kneed his horse about, his back to the officer. "Bring me the *alcalde,*" he said to a nervous peasant standing nearby.

Moments later a thin, balding man emerged from a doorway and shuffled toward Jack on aged legs.

"*Sí, señor?* I am Juan Cortina, *alcalde* of Laredo. What is it you wish?"

"Only to bring you this message, Juan Cortina. Should any Mexican troops use your town as a base to invade Texas, or should you house any bandits who raid our citizens, your town will be sacked and burned. This is no threat, Mayor Cortina. It is the promise of the Texas Rangers."

Jack wheeled his mount and left Laredo at a lazy trot, the other Rangers falling in behind. At his side Jack heard Thad Green's sigh of relief.

"Captain, how on God's earth did you know we could pull that off without getting killed?"

Jack glanced at the young Ranger. "The nature of the enemy, Thad. A Mexican soldier prepared for battle and knowing one's coming will put up a fight. That same soldier facing something totally unexpected won't know what to do. So we approach the Mexican the same way we do the Comanche—we do exactly the opposite of what *he* would do if he were in our boots. Keep an enemy confused and you've won the battle. Win enough battles and you win the war."

Jack fell silent for a few minutes, letting Thad Green chew on another bite of his education as a Texas Ranger.

"Thad, there's one more thing. When the war comes, never surrender to a Mexican, no matter what he promises. Texas has lost more men to Mexican treachery than to all their lances and guns. If you're going to be shot anyway, you might as well make them pay the price."

"Captain, are you sure there will be a war?"

"Yes. There's no way around it, Thad. There *will* be a war. It's only a matter of when."

SEVEN

San Antonio
April 1841

Jack Hays listened to the distant rumble of thunder from the spring storm as it moved away toward the northeast. Water still dripped from the eaves of the Ranger company headquarters, the gentle peck of the drops on the mud of the street soothing to the ears.

Across the table littered with scraps of leather and a stripped Paterson Colt, Sam Walker sat in a straight-backed chair, a feather pillow stuffed between the chair slats and his lower back.

"Thunderstorm sounds halfway nice if a man isn't caught in it horseback," Walker said. "This is the first one in a year I can remember riding out inside and dry instead of on a saddle with my butt getting raw."

Jack tugged a stitch tight on the holster taking shape under his fingers. "Does seem like we've been on patrol forever, Sam. How's the back?"

Walker shifted his weight and winced. "Better. Still stings some, but Doc Robinson says it's starting to heal. I'll be back in the saddle before long. A hell of a lot sooner than the Comanche that stuck me." A distant look settled in the Ranger's blue eyes. "Jack, that was one fine scrap."

Jack grunted in agreement and tied off the final stitch in the holster. It had been a good fight by Ranger standards. A war party of ten Indians wiped out after twenty miles of tracking and a quick, bloody fight on the banks of a muddy creek. That bunch had killed their last settler. They had almost killed Sam, too; one warrior had managed to get a lance in Walker's lower back, but it had sliced through the muscle above the hipbone instead of going straight in. The Comanche stopped a pistol ball with his forehead for his troubles. Sam Walker had a tendency to get mad when somebody lanced him.

The Rangers had only one other injury, and that was something of a fluke. Young Thad Green had started to pull his Colt from the waistband of his pants when the exposed trigger started to drop, snagged and the gun went off. Thad caught a nasty powder burn across his thigh and, later, some serious ribbing from the other Rangers. "At least it wasn't pointed straight down," Thad had said. "Man could lose some important equipment that way, and I'm not through using mine yet."

The first thing Thad had done after taking care of his horse and swabbing a little bacon grease on the powder burn was to design a belt holster for the Paterson so nobody else would lose any hide by accident. Thad's holster carried the Colt high on the belt so that it didn't interfere with mounting and riding a horse. A flap at the top kept the weapon dry and protected it from dust. Thad also modified an infantry-style ammunition pouch to ride behind the holster. The pouch held a spare loaded cylinder, powder, caps, balls, and a tamping rod for reloading. The Rangers also carried a shoulder rig with extra ammunition. If a man's horse got knocked down or bucked him off, at least he would have some reserve firepower at hand. Most of the Rangers now wore two of Thad's holsters, one on each side of his belt.

Jack was finishing his second one. He would wear it cross-draw style so he wouldn't have to switch the bridle reins to his right hand to pull the second gun. He slipped his Paterson in and out of the holster a couple of times until he was satisfied with the fit and feel. He cocked an eyebrow at Sam Walker. The Ranger's face had slipped into a frown as he stared at the stripped-down pistol on the table before him. Jack knew what Sam was thinking. The Rangers hadn't had the Patersons a week before they started figuring out ways to improve it. The Paterson had been the main talk around the camp fires, pushing aside discussions of Indians and Mexicans, and even women. Jack welcomed the diversion for two reasons. First, the pistol was the main tool of the Ranger trade. Second, it kept him from thinking too much about Susan Calvert.

"Got it figured out, Sam?"

"Got a start on it. We know the Texas Model's too light, too flimsy for hard use. The old horse pistols, you could whack somebody up beside the head and they'd drop like you'd hit them with an axe. Hit somebody with this thing and all you do is wreck the gun. It needs a lot more heft."

Jack grunted in rueful agreement. He had been out another sixty dollars of his own money for repairs to the Patersons already. The gun just couldn't take the abuse a Ranger put it through.

Walker pulled an oft-folded paper and a pencil stub from his shirt pocket. The pencil scratched. Sam looked up. "Needs more muscle on the front end, too," he said. "I busted a Comanche square in the chest from forty yards and he didn't go down. Thirty-four just doesn't pack enough wallop. We need a man-stopper, Jack. At least a forty-four caliber."

Jack pulled one of his Patersons and hefted the weapon. It never had felt quite right to the hand. "If we eliminate the bulge at the base of the grip and put a little more curve on the back-strap, the balance would be a lot better."

Sam nodded, scribbled another note and a sketch, then paused, chewing on the end of the pencil. "Main thing we need is something we don't have to take apart to reload. Hell of a chore for a man on horseback when a Comanche's coming at him. You're the engineer, Jack. You have any ideas on that?"

Jack shoved the pistol back into its holster. "Gun design isn't my specialty, but I do have an idea, Sam. Turn the problem over to the expert. When you're well enough to travel, I'd like you to go back east. Meet with Sam Colt. Tell him he's got a fine weapon, but we need a better one. Let him know what we want and let's see if he can come up with it. Lamar's authorized the Rangers to buy five hundred of them, and I expect he'll get plenty of orders for an improved Colt."

Sam Walker's face brightened. "I can heal on the way up and back. It isn't much worse than a scratch, anyway."

"No, Sam. Let's don't take any chances. We can get by with the Texas Model for a spell, and I don't want to lose you to an infection or something from rushing it. It'll wait until you've healed."

The conversation trailed off at the sound of hooves pounding through the mud outside. Jack was on his feet and at the door in two strides.

Bigfoot Wallace yanked his horse to a stop a few feet from the door. "Problem in Laredo again, Jack," Wallace said. "Agaton's damn bandits bushwhacked some teamsters just north of the Navarro Ranch. Killed the traders and headed on into Laredo. One of our Mexican *amigos* there sent word that they're still in town."

Jack reached for his pistol belt. "Get on the bell rope, Bigfoot, and see how many men we can raise. I'm getting a little tired of these bandits."

Sam Walker winced as he started to rise. Jack put a hand on his shoulder and gently eased him back into the chair. "Oh, hell, Jack. I can ride."

"Sam, you're not going anywhere until that back is healed. Stay here of your own accord or I'll lay a chunk of firewood alongside your hard head."

Walker grumbled, but stayed in the chair.

A half hour later Jack surveyed his company. He had eight Rangers who hadn't been out on patrol, Samuel Maverick and three other American merchants who had a heavy stake in the border trade and thirteen Mexican Texans led by businessman Antonio Perez.

"Antonio, thank you for coming," Jack said.

Anger smouldered in Antonio Perez's dark brown eyes. "Find us these bandits, Captain Jack. And a tree. We brought our own ropes."

Jack Hays waved his men to a stop ten miles from Laredo and glared toward the group of approaching horsemen.

They were Mexican mounted infantry, about forty strong, commanded by a tall, lean man in the uniform of a captain.

"Antonio," Jack said to the man at his side, "do you know this captain?"

"By last name only. Garcia. He is not fond of *gringos* or Mexicans who ride with them. There is a rumor that he is an ally of Agaton."

A bugle sounded from the approaching column. The Mexican dragoons spurred their mounts into a slow trot toward the Texans. Jack lifted the flap on his holster and palmed the Colt. He heard the rustle of leather and the metallic *click* of hammers being pulled to full cock on pistols, shotguns and rifles behind him. Perez pulled his own rifle. "What is your wish, Captain Jack?"

"They'll be expecting us to fort up. So we'll charge them as soon as the dragoons dismount."

The Mexican soldiers rode to within a hundred yards. Garcia, in his gaudy uniform, called out: "Surrender or be slaughtered, *gringos!*"

Jack glanced at Bigfoot Wallace. "Answer them for us, Bigfoot," Jack said calmly.

Wallace nodded. "Glad to, Captain." He spat a stream of tobacco juice, shifted the chew to his other cheek and raised his voice. "Go to hell, you goddamn dog-eatin' sons of Nogales whores!"

The Mexican captain screamed an outraged obscenity. The bugle sounded again. Dragoons swung from their horses, heavy rifles in hand.

"Now! Charge them!" Jack yelled.

The thunder of Texas hooves caught the Mexican troops by surprise. A ragged volley of hurried shots went wild over the Texans' heads. Jack noticed the captain had not dismounted, and two of the dragoons had quickly climbed back into their saddles. The Texans smashed into the Mexican line, the sharp bark of revolvers mingling with the heavy blast of rifles and deep cough of shotguns, the cries of startled men and shrieks of the wounded.

The battle ended with the Texans' charge. The dragoons grounded their weapons in surrender, pleading for quarter. Captain Garcia and the two men who had remounted were spurring their horses back toward Laredo.

Jack took a quick inventory of his own ranks and breathed a

sigh of relief. The San Antonio force was unscathed. The Mexicans had fared considerably less well. Three dragoons lay dead and three others were seriously wounded. Twenty-five were prisoners. The Texans had captured twenty-eight horses, along with saddles and bridles, firearms, powder and lead.

"Well, Jack, what next?"

Jack glanced at Bigfoot Wallace. "We haven't caught our bandits yet, Bigfoot. We're going into Laredo."

Jack left a force to guard the prisoners—after convincing Antonio Perez it would not be necessary to shoot them—and led his group toward Laredo.

A mile from town the *alcalde* met them astride a burro, a white flag held at shoulder level. The old man's gaze dropped as he met Jack's cold stare. He remembered the Ranger captain's last visit to Laredo.

"Please, señor," the Laredo mayor pleaded, "I beg you—do not destroy my poor town."

"I made you a promise last time," Jack said. "You were warned. Yet you offered shelter to the bandit Agaton."

"*Señor capitán,* the people of Laredo had no choice. Agaton would have killed us all. I beseech you in the name of God, spare my people!"

Jack let the silence and the tension build for several heartbeats, then shrugged. "Very well, *alcalde.* I will give you one more chance. Bring me the bandit Agaton and the goods he stole. Then the Texas Rangers will spare your people. You have five hours."

"*Señor capitán,* I—"

"You are wasting time, *alcalde.*"

Jack waited until the old man on the burro had grown small in the distance, then dismounted to wait.

Four hours later, the bandit's body dangled from a cottonwood tree, Perez's *riata* digging deep into his neck.

"It is enough, *alcalde,*" Jack told the nervous Laredo mayor. "You have given us the bandit and returned the stolen goods. We will spare your town. This time." Jack turned to Bigfoot Wallace and waved a hand toward the body swaying in the breeze. "Let him down, Bigfoot, and bring Señor Perez's rope. We have some prisoners to deliver to San Antonio."

"Leave the body," Perez called. "It will be a reminder to other bandits. I have plenty of *riatas.*" Perez turned to Jack. "Captain Jack, I do not know how the peons of Laredo found the courage to capture Agaton and deliver him to you."

Jack toed the stirrup and swung aboard his sorrel. "Fear, Antonio. They now fear the Rangers more than they fear their own bandits. It's what I want. I want them to fear us more than the devil himself." He reined his horse back toward home.

San Antonio
September 1841

Jack Hays wiped the last trace of lather from his chin, dried the keen blade of the straight razor and slipped it back into its leather pouch.

He felt human again for the first time in weeks. *At least I don't smell like a he-goat at breeding time,* he thought. A bath and a shave could wash away the miles, even a little bit of the exhaustion, and the body felt better. It was too bad the same activities couldn't cleanse the mind of worry.

He slipped into a fresh shirt, strode to the window of his combination home and office and let his gaze drift across the wind-whipped dust of the street. Once again the rains had forsaken the Texas frontier. A relentless sun blazed overhead, grinding through the ceaseless southwest wind which sucked the last traces of moisture from the soil and baked the streams dry. The grass was dry and brittle on the plains to the north and west. *It's as if civilization as we know it has bumped straight into the gates of Hell,* Jack thought.

Still, the settlers came.

Farmers in search of land poured into the valleys and along the rivers near San Antonio and Austin, filled with optimism and faith that the Lord would provide.

The Lord seemed busy elsewhere. He had certainly had little time for Texas of late. And, Jack knew, it was about to get worse. Lamar's Santa Fe Expedition had been a miserable failure. The

Texans had endured the tortures of thirst, heat, wind and Indians. Many graves now marked their passage across the Llano Estacado. Santa Fe had welcomed the tattered force Mexican style. The survivors of the brutal trek were imprisoned. Occasionally, one was shot, more as an example than for punishment of any crime.

Lamar had made his claim annexing the Californias to Texas. The small but efficient Texas Navy plied the waters of the Gulf, a threat to Mexican commerce. More commercial treaties had been signed between Texas, Great Britain, France, Belgium and the Netherlands, acts not lost on the government of Mexico. Worst of all, Santa Anna had returned from exile and regained power.

The wind from the south blew more than just dust, Jack knew. It was the wind of war. Lamar had done his job well. There was little doubt now that Lamar would lose the election, but there wasn't much that Sam Houston could do to stop the tide. Any day now Jack expected to look up and see a battalion of Mexican soldiers marching through the plaza at San Antonio.

As if the Mexico troubles weren't enough, Comanche raiders continued to rape and plunder along the frontier. Jack could count on one hand the number of days he and his men had not been on patrol, looking for Mexicans, Indians or both, plagued by heat, thirst, dense swarms of deer flies that tormented men and horses alike, or eaten alive by hordes of mosquitoes from the bogs and seeps that still held stagnant water. Against the Mexicans and the Indians, Jack had less than a hundred men at his call. The Republic had no funds to supply and equip more Rangers. The treaties with the European countries did not include any hard currency loans.

Jack turned from the window. The hot breath of the wind already had left his fresh shirt soaked with sweat. He strode to the desk, found paper and pen, and chewed on the staff for several minutes. Writing a report was one thing; writing a letter to a woman was another bear to wrestle. Finally, his thoughts in order, he began to write.

Dear Miss Calvert,

Please forgive my delay in answering your most welcome letter. I have just today returned from several days afield.

Jack fought back the urge to write that he had carried her letter throughout the long patrol, and had read it many times— as much to hold something she had touched as for the contents, which he could recite from memory. That would be much too forward.

I must tell you that conditions have worsened in Texas since last we spoke. I fear an invasion from Mexico is imminent, and the Comanches continue to make life a tenuous thing here on the frontier.

It is not only my wish to discourage you from moving to Seguin, it is my duty to do so. I beg you, please wait a few more months. I cannot bear the thought of you and yours falling into the hands of the Mexicans or Comanches.

Thank you for inquiring as to my health; it is fine, as I pray may be your own. Please give my regards to your family.
Yr Obt Svt
JOHN COFFEE HAYS
Ranger Hq, San Antonio

Jack breathed gently on the last few lines to help the ink dry. *Dammit, Jack,* he scolded himself, *you didn't have the guts to tell her all the things you really wanted to say.* He folded the letter, slipped it into the envelope with the Nacogdoches address and hoped it would reach her. The Texas mails sometimes went awry, and he couldn't justify sending a courier with a personal message.

Twenty minutes later, Jack Hays left the letter at the general store, which doubled as post office, and returned to the column of men waiting outside. He swung into the saddle. "Well, gentlemen," he said, "you've had your one night's rest and your bath for the month. Let's go hunt up some Indians."

Luck had run out for the two homesteader families on the banks of the Sabinal River. But if it was any consolation to them, luck was about to run out on a band of Comanches, Jack Hays promised the broken and mutilated bodies near the embers of the cabins.

Smoke still rose from the wreckage. An occasional wisp of flame flicked a snake tongue along the charred cottonwood logs that once had been a home. Jack saw at a glance that the settlers had put up a bitter fight.

"Bury them now, Jack?"

Jack glanced at Ben McCulloch and shook his head. "It wouldn't help them any. And we've got a hot trail to follow. Let's gather some Comanches first." Jack motioned the patrol forward. Ben took the point, riding the track at an easy trot. After a mile he returned to the column.

"They're headed for Uvalde Canyon, Jack. Not more than a couple hours' lead on us."

Jack knew the country well. Beyond its half-mile-wide mouth, Uvalde Canyon narrowed sharply as it twisted into the hills beyond. There were only two ways out of the canyon, through the mouth over the narrow pass to the northwest.

"Ben, take ten men with you," Jack said. "Circle around the canyon and get in front of the Comanches at the pass. Turn them back to us. There's a heavy thicket in the middle of the canyon. We'll run them into that thicket, and we won't let them out alive."

Thad Green waited until Ben's group disappeared from view, then nudged his horse alongside Jack. "Why the thicket, Captain? Wouldn't it be easier to just ride them down in the open?"

"No, Thad. A Comanche's a tough man on horseback, but get him afoot and it takes some of the starch out of his breechclout. A bow's all but useless in a heavy thicket. Hangs up on the branches, limbs get in the way of the arrows. On top of which, a Comanche doesn't like to fight where he can't see all around. He's a Plains warrior, not a forest Indian." Jack waved the remainder of his Ranger column forward at the trot.

The Comanche warrior's death song wailed above the dense thicket. Jack Hays thumbed the hammer of the sawed-off ten-gauge shotgun and waited. He had plenty of time to wait. It was the Indian's move. The six-hour battle in the thicket had come down to one man against another. One of them wouldn't leave.

The warrior couldn't run. There was nowhere to go. Jack's Rangers had the thicket surrounded; their rifles had already taken down four Indians who had tried to run rather than fight in that heavy tangle of brush and stunted trees.

Eleven Indians and three Rangers had gone into the thicket. Big Bill Davis and Thad Green had been wounded in the bloody close-quarter fighting. Jack had banished them from the brush to the safety of Ranger lines and Doc Robinson's ministrations.

The barrel of Jack's shotgun was still warm to the touch. The scattergun had taken down three Indians, and the Paterson Colt in Jack's holster dropped another. He used the pistol only when he hadn't time to reload the shotgun. The Indians had fought well, with the desperation of trapped animals, and accepted death bravely when it came. Jack wondered if the remaining Comanche's death song was meant for personal salvation or if it were being sung for one Ranger captain.

The Comanche chant abruptly ended. Silence fell heavy over the brush, broken only by the drone of flies and piercing *chirr* of cicadas resuming their chorus after the gunshots died. A Mexican jay squawked and fluttered, indignant at the intrusion into his thicket home. The dim tree-filtered light flashed on the bird's green feathers.

Jack crouched in a shallow depression, his senses acute. He felt the steady thump of his heart against his ribs; the veins of a leaf quavering near his face stood out in sharp relief. Jack knew the last Comanche carried a firearm, an ancient flintlock rifle. Jack directed most of his attention to his right; most Comanches on the stalk tended to circle to their own left.

The faint crack of a twig sounded at Jack's left. The warrior had outguessed him. Jack whirled, shotgun at hip level—and stared into the vermilion-streaked face of the Comanche less than twenty feet away. The Indian's rifle pointed at Jack's breast. Jack threw himself to his right and felt the jolt of a heavy ball against his left shoulder as the rifle blast rattled the leaves. He fired both barrels of the shotgun. The buckshot charge slammed into the warrior's belly and hurled him backward, the flintlock spinning away. Jack scrambled to his feet, drew his Paterson and moved cautiously toward the Indian.

Life still flickered in the deep black eyes. The Comanche reached weakly toward the knife at his belt. Jack aimed his handgun and fired, putting the gut-shot Indian out of his misery. He took the time to holster the pistol and reload the shotgun before glancing at his shoulder. The ball had nicked the thick muscle just below the shoulder seam of his shirt. Jack realized with a start it was the first time he had been wounded in battle, and at the same time sighed in relief. It was little more than a shallow gouge. It didn't even hurt much. Jack made his way to the edge of the thicket. He waved the shotgun overhead until he was sure he wouldn't be shot by mistake by his own men, then strode into the open.

Ben McCulloch spurred his big bay to Jack's side and stepped from the saddle before the horse had finished his sliding stop. "You hit, Jack?"

"Nothing serious. Ruined a new four-bit shirt is about all. The others?"

"They'll make it. You want a ride?"

"No, thanks. I'll stretch my legs a bit. How'd we do, Ben?"

"Damn well, I'd say. We nailed five of them on the way in. One got away when we first jumped them. I got a rifle ball in him, but near as I can tell I just hit him in the cheek of the ass. Want to hunt him down? He isn't likely to be riding very fast."

Jack shook his head. "Let him go. He can help us more by spreading talk of the bad medicine Rangers than by getting himself dead."

Jack's shoulder was beginning to throb, more of a nuisance than a real pain, as they walked up to the gathering of Rangers.

Doc Robinson was removing an arrow that had gone through Thad Green's thigh. The doctor cut through the shaft on the feathered end, grabbed the bloodied point and yanked. Green winced but didn't cry out. Jack saw with relief that the blood from Thad's leg wasn't coming in spurts. That meant no arteries had been hit. At least the young Ranger wouldn't bleed to death.

"Thad, son, I don't know what we're going to do with you," Jack said with a smile. "You don't learn to duck, I'll be burying you a piece at a time for months. Lose part of an ear, almost shoot off your own *cojones* and now you step in front of a Comanche arrow."

The pale-faced Thad managed a weak grin. "Guess I'm slowing down in my old age. Looks like you forgot to duck, too, Captain."

"I did duck, Thad, or I'd have caught that one in the chest instead of losing a little chunk of shoulder. You hurting?"

"Hell, yes, Captain. Not as bad as old Bill, though." Thad nodded toward Bill Davis. The big man sat propped against a small boulder, his belly swathed in bandages. "Fell on his knife, I think."

"Damn you, Thad! You know better than that," Davis howled in indignation. "Fell on my knife, hell! Comanche biggern' I am tried to gut me. He didn't get the job done, so I cut his throat."

Jack knelt beside the big man. "How bad is it, Bill?"

Doc Robinson answered as he wiped blood from his hands on his pants leg. "Not bad. Blade sliced across a few belly muscles. An inch deeper and Bill here would be leaking biscuits along about now. I stitched him up. He cussed me out something fierce."

Davis muttered something about a damned old broken-down reprobate sawbones who'd have done everybody a favor if he'd decided to be a barber, but he was grinning when he said it.

Satisfied that all that could be done for his men had been done, Jack let Robinson tend his shoulder wound. "Can Thad and Bill ride, Doc?"

"Yes. As long as they take it slow and easy."

Jack glanced at the lowering sun. "It's been a long day, but we're not through yet. We've some bodies to bury, men. We can make the Sabinal homesteads by dark, then go home in the morning."

EIGHT

San Antonio
December 1841

Jack Hays leaned against a wall in the main hall of Antonio Perez's spacious home and watched the dancers whirl about the
hardwood floor to the strains of a brassy Mexican band.

Colorful *piñatas* dangled by strings from the rafters, waiting
only the signal that would send blindfolded children flailing with
sticks to break the containers and grab at the candy and other
prizes which tumbled out. Bright streamers vied with the *piñatas*
for space above the crowded dance floor. Tables heavy with food
and drink pulled a knot of people toward one end of the hall.

Jack had given up trying to absorb the festive mood. The
Christmas spirit came from within. Jack admitted his withins
were without this year, only a void where the happier side of his
nature should have been.

He politely ignored the inviting glances from several pretty
señoritas seated along the wall awaiting a dancing partner, or
perhaps a more serious suitor for the night. He couldn't help
looking for someone who wasn't there. The scent of lilac water
and burnished brown hair, the feel of Susan Calvert's small, firm
waist beneath his hand were still strong in his memory. *Where
would she be tonight,* he wondered. *Who would she be dancing and
laughing with?* Jack told himself he had no claim to Susan, but
he couldn't put the thought of her from his mind.

The other Rangers at Antonio Perez's Christmas *baile* did not share Jack's loneliness. Thad Green still favored the wounded leg, but he never missed a dance. Neither did Bill Davis. The cut across his belly had healed, and Jack doubted the young señorita in Bill's arms for yet another turn on the dance floor would mind when she saw the scar later. Jack was willing to wager she would see it.

Even Bigfoot Wallace was there, wearing clean buckskins for a change, whooping and trying his hand at every dance that came along. Jack idly wondered how those huge feet that could move without sound through dry leaves and dead grass could get in each other's way on a smooth floor—

"Captain Jack, I must speak with you," Antonio Perez said softly at Jack's side, "in private." The merchant's somber expression belied his festive holiday clothing. He wore the expensive formal silver-studded and heavily embroidered black pants and vest of the Mexican *vaquero*. Perez led the way to a small but comfortable study, down the corridor from the ballroom. He waved Jack into a soft leather chair and perched on the edge of an ornately carved wood desk.

"I hate to add to your worries at this time of celebration," Perez said, "but I have today received messages from a friend in Mexico City I must bring to your attention. Santa Anna is building his armies rapidly, moving troops and supplies toward northern Mexico. He is still in a rage over the Santa Fe Expedition. I fear he has planned his revenge."

"Santa Anna will invade us, Antonio. We have accepted that as a fact for some time. The only question is when."

"This my informant could not say, Jack. He could only say he thought it would be soon." Perez strode to a window, stared for a moment into the darkness. "I think spring," he said. "April, perhaps. Maybe March if the rains come between the Nueces and the Rio Grande. No man can move an army across the Mustang Desert until the rains bring grass and replenish the few water holes."

Jack rose and paced the floor for a minute in silence. "Antonio," he said, "I made a promise to President Lamar. I promised we would hold San Antonio. I think I've made a promise I can't keep."

Antonio Perez turned to Jack and smiled in reassurance. "We will find a way, Jack Hays. We have beaten Santa Anna once. He can be beaten again. We will save Texas despite our own politicians." Antonio offered a hand. "I will place my men at your call. Their skins may be dark, but they are as much Texas *gringo* as I am myself."

Jack gripped Antonio's hand. He seemed to draw new strength from the Mexican Texan. "Thank you, Antonio. I am pleased to call you friend."

Antonio placed his free hand on Jack's shoulder. "Then come back to the *baile* with me, my friend. It is time to loose the children upon the *piñatas.*" Antonio laughed, a deep, guttural expression of pleasure. "If you think we are going to have a war, wait until you see the battle that develops when the *piñatas* break."

Goliad
March 1842

Jack Hays ground his fingers into the pommel of his saddle until his knuckles ached, trying to squeeze his frustration into the well-worn leather.

It didn't help.

A mile below Jack's vantage point on a low rise north of Goliad, the snake and eagle flag fluttered above the old mission. General Rafael Vasquez's troops, a thousand strong, went casually about their business on the plain where Texas patriots had been coldly executed only a few years before. And there wasn't one damn thing Jack Hays could do about it.

The ghosts of Goliad seemed to mock him from the shadows. Jack's force of eighty-six Rangers and volunteers had fallen back from San Antonio, retreated from Refugio, and now Vasquez had taken Goliad without a shot fired.

The constant retreat galled Jack Hays. The idea of Mexican soldiers relieving themselves on the very ground where Texans had bled and died almost pushed him beyond reason and into rage and foolishness. Even now he yearned to call the charge,

smash into the enemy, make them pay a heavy price for their
audacity. Again he held the impulse in check, subordinating his
emotions to cold logic. As good as his Rangers were, it would be
suicide to attack a thousand well-armed, professional soldiers
commanded by perhaps the best field general to wear a Mexican
uniform.

All he could do was watch and wait.

Ben McCulloch reined his big roan to a stop at Jack's side. The
animal's neck and shoulders were soaked with sweat and
streaked in foamy lather. The roan's head drooped, nostrils
flared as its lungs heaved for air. Ben swung down and loosened
the girth before turning to Jack.

"There isn't a supply train anywhere," Ben said, rubbing a
hand across his saddle-numbed buttocks. "We've scouted clear
to Laredo and back, and not one sign or track. We've had riders
around Vasquez's bunch since before San Antonio. No reinforcements on the way, no supply train, no field artillery."

Jack stared toward the Mexican Army camp. "And Vasquez
didn't sack San Antonio. Not a single store looted, not a white
woman molested. He didn't take any Texans prisoner. I couldn't
figure for sure what he's up to—until now. Ben, this is no invasion. It's just Santa Anna's way of sending us a message. Or feeling us out to see how we'd react."

Ben shifted his tobacco chew to the other cheek and spat.
"Could be."

"The question is, how much farther can Vasquez go? When
his supply wagons are half empty, he'll have to turn back."

Ben glanced at the setting sun. "Come full dark, I can sure as
hell find out."

"That would be chancy, Ben. Vasquez is no fool. He's got a
solid perimeter and double pickets. A quarter of his people are
awake and on duty at any one time."

Ben McCulloch snorted. "Jack, I can pass for a Mexican in the
dark. And when it gets to the point I can't go into an enemy
camp and get back out again, just pull a pistol and shoot me. I
wouldn't be worth weak piss as a Ranger then, anyway."

"All right, Ben. But keep your backside down. You need some
help?"

"Nope. There's not but a thousand or so of 'em. Won't even break a sweat."

Ben returned two hours before daybreak, squatted before Jack's small fire and swept the oversized Mexican hat from his head. He wore the rough clothing of a Mexican teamster, even down to the bullwhip over his shoulder. Jack didn't ask him where he got the outfit. He waited patiently as McCulloch sliced a fresh chew from his plug, settled the tobacco comfortably in a cheek and waved the point of his knife toward the fires below.

"Vasquez is going to be on thin rations soon, Jack. Half the supply wagons are empty. But I can go you one better. Got a conversation going with a thirsty oxcart handler over a pint of tequila I been carrying for weeks. Come daylight, Vasquez starts back to Mexico."

Jack felt the sense of helplessness that had dogged him for more than a week finally drop away.

"Jack, you think we ought to maybe kick old Vasquez in the butt a little, just to help him on his way?"

"There's nothing I'd like better, Ben. But Vasquez hasn't harmed any Texans yet. I'd rather not give him the chance. Don't kick a sleeping dog and nobody gets bit. That doesn't mean we won't nip at his heels a little until he leaves Texas. Messages go both ways."

Jack Hays watched as the last of General Rafael Vasquez's troops sloshed across the shallow Nueces onto Mexican soil.

He could almost hear a collective sigh of relief from the two companies of dragoons assigned by Vasquez as a rear guard during the withdrawal. The number of Texans dogging Vasquez's retreat had grown by the day as word of the invasion spread. Jack had forbidden an attack along the way; he had almost two hundred men under his command now, most of them volunteers, and all chafing to draw Mexican blood. But he had kept the more reckless Texans in check. He was still heavily outnumbered. If he attacked, Vasquez could wheel his troops, launch a counterstrike and overwhelm the Texans.

It was enough that the Rangers and volunteers had kept a steady pressure on Vasquez during his retreat. The Texans stayed just out of rifle range, but always at Vasquez's heels, menacing the rear guard, turning back foraging and hunting parties, forcing Vasquez to march his men on half rations. Several times the Mexican soldiers had seemed ready to bolt, but Vasquez's officers had maintained discipline. A lesser commander might have lost control.

He glanced along the line of tight faces and hard eyes that made up the Ranger force, now spread along the Texas bank of the Nueces. *Vasquez did what he came to do, and no one was hurt,* Jack thought, *but we've sent our own message to Santa Anna. You can't intimidate a Texan that easily.*

"Well, Jack, looks like it's over."

Jack studied Ben McCulloch's bearded face, the blue eyes bloodshot from lack of sleep. Ben looked disappointed. Jack understood. He had wanted a fight himself, but on terms more to his own liking. "Over for now, Ben," he said. "But I'd bet a good horse against a one-eyed mule they'll be back. And next time it won't be just a show of force." Jack shifted his weight in the saddle to ease the ache in his knees. He had been horseback for fourteen or more hours a day for a week.

It was time to send the volunteers home, with an expression of thanks. And to ask them to keep their guns and horses handy for when the Mexicans came back. *It won't be so easy next time,* he reminded himself, *for either side.*

San Antonio
July 1842

The mockingbird outside Jack Hays's window embellished her serenade with a series of raucous squawks reminiscent of a magpie cry, then abruptly fell silent as if embarrassed that she had stooped to such a low in her search for fresh material.

A slight smile lifted the corners of Jack's mouth. He had grown fond of the mockingbird's daily—and sometimes nightlong—serenade. The bird was a friend now. Jack had watched her raise nestlings for two seasons, frazzling her feathers in her attempts to keep her ravenous babies fed, and swooping down to knock fur from the heads of the occasional cat or dog that wandered too close to the nest.

She was about the only light to shine on Jack Hays's life this summer.

He waited until the bird had regained her poise and burst into a new repetitive melody, then turned his attention back to the desk. It overflowed with official reports, formal and informal letters from other Texas outposts and beyond, newspaper clippings, Jack's own notes regarding supplies and equipment to be bought, begged or borrowed, his company ledger with eighty-five Ranger names on the roll.

Jack had begun to hate that desk. He tolerated it as a necessity of command. Information was as valuable as a pistol to a Ranger. Jack read through two more reports, then heaved himself from the hard wooden chair.

His hip still protested every movement. The deep bruise was a long time healing, it seemed. Judas had bucked him off again, the third time this month. It was a hard fall. Jack's dignity was damaged more than his hip. *That damn horse is going to do something the Comanches and Mexicans haven't been able to do,* Jack grumbled inwardly; *the fool is going to kill me one of these days.*

They had been through a lot together, the Ranger and the lanky sorrel. But Judas was showing signs of wear and tear from the long, hard miles and the heated battles. He was going on eleven, now, old by frontier standards. Texas was pure hell on horses. One more patrol, Jack promised, and he would retire Judas. The cranky, unpredictable animal had earned a long rest. *But, by God, not after you've won the last hand, you thick-headed, Roman-nosed idiot.*

Jack forced his mind back to the situation at hand. It wasn't good.

The Vasquez invasion had set off a howl of outrage across Texas and beyond. Houston's own Peace Party Congress had passed a declaration of war on Mexico. Houston just as promptly vetoed the measure, and made the veto stick despite the panther squawls of the populace.

Santa Anna, under growing pressure from diplomats of the United States, Texas and numerous foreign governments, had relented and released the Santa Fe Expedition survivors. Their stories of starvation, mistreatment and random executions fanned new fires of Texas hate for Mexico.

Houston had even signed a peace treaty with the Southern Comanches. The treaty hadn't meant beans to the Panetekas. The raids had slacked, but Jack knew it was from fear of the Rangers, not from a mark made on paper. The Panetekas had been content of late with stealing a few head of livestock, and only a couple of settlers had been killed.

Further, Jack had still received no new funds to boost his Ranger force. Many of the few men he had were now scattered along the frontier, patrolling the edges of Comanche country and the border with Mexico.

Texas's troubles went beyond Mexico and Comancheria. The Republic's efforts to become part of the United States had again been stalled by the free-staters. This time, the fight had been closer. Most of the United States favored Texas annexation, at least as a territory if not a state. The main opposition came from the Northeastern states, and at the moment they held the whip hand in Congress.

"Politicians," Jack groused aloud, "are a royal pain in the ass."

He turned as the door swung open and felt a grin spread over his face as a familiar figure stepped into the room.

"Sam Walker! I'd about decided you liked New York better than Texas. Welcome home." He extended a hand.

Walker's grin was as wide as Jack's own. "It's good to be back, Jack. Damn, there isn't room in the big city to cuss a cat." Walker released Jack's hand, swept a new silver beaver hat from his head and tossed it onto a chair. "Understand I missed some fun. I've heard so many wild tales I don't know who to believe. Except you. Want to tell me about it?"

"Don't know as you could call it fun, Sam. I'll fill you in later. First, how did the meeting with Colt go?"

Walker held out a hand, palm up, index finger extended, thumb poised as if to cock an unseen hammer. "You'll like it, Jack. Sam Colt's a fine hand with gun design. It'll have everything we wanted and then some. Sam's excited about it, too. He took one last look at the design we finally settled on and almost drooled on the sketches. Said it would make him almost as famous as it will the Rangers."

"When can we expect the guns?"

"Just as soon as Eli Whitney's plant can turn them out. Colt doesn't have a plant of his own yet." The grin faded from Walker's face. "Jack, there's something else—well, it wasn't my idea—"

"Go ahead, Sam. Spit it out. I've gotten used to bad news."

"Colonel Colt insisted on calling the new handgun the Walker Model. I tried to convince him it ought to be named the Hays Model."

Jack chuckled in relief. "I thought you were going to tell me some bad news, Sam. You've earned the honor. I just hope the guns get here before the Mexicans do."

Walker raised an eyebrow. "That bad, is it?"

Jack nodded toward a chair. "Sit down, and I'll tell you why I think we're going to be up to our butts in Santa Anna's boys. Maybe sooner than anybody expects."

NINE

Nueces River
September 1842

Jack Hays knelt on one knee amid the broad track left by the Mexican Army force. The trail was well off the main roads. It twisted between the hills, kept to the low country, but always threaded back to the same general heading. Toward San Antonio.

At Jack's side, Bigfoot Wallace poked a stick into a pile of horse droppings and studied the contents. "Two days ago, moving fast. Would have raised dust we could have spotted if it hadn't been for that rainstorm. They'll be in San'tone by now."

Jack slapped his fist into a thigh in disgust. "Dammit, Bigfoot, they've caught me asleep again. How on God's green earth can any Ranger *not* find a whole Mexican army until it's too late?"

Wallace spat the worked-over tobacco cud from his mouth and carved a fresh chew from a plug. "No need thrashin' yourself over it. Big country out here."

Jack's self-disgust faded as quickly as it had flared. The big frontiersman was right. Nothing could be done about what had already happened. Jack's thoughts raced forward to San Antonio. There was no way Sam Walker could hold the city, not with less than forty men against an army. The other Rangers were scattered on patrols from below the Frio to above the Guadalupe.

"Sam Walker ain't no idiot," Bigfoot said, as though reading Jack's mind. "He'll pull back. My guess would be Seguin. Best spot to watch the country from."

Thad Green trotted up on his long-legged bay. "They have a cannon with them, Captain. Tracks say it's probably a three-pounder. And there's too many heavy wagons to count, along with a mess of carts."

"Then they mean business this time." Jack abruptly stood and swung back into the saddle. "Thad, cut south of San Antonio. Get word to Matthew Caldwell at Gonzales, tell him we need every man we can get. We'll meet at Seguin."

Green didn't stop to ask questions. He wheeled his horse and left at a fast trot.

Jack turned to the two other riders on the patrol. "Bill, take a turn up the Guadalupe country. Gather all our men you can find and anybody else that has a gun and a horse. Barney, ride for Victoria and spread the word." Davis nodded and turned his mount to the north; Barney Randall pointed his long-legged chestnut southeast.

"What you want from me, Jack?"

"Come with me, Bigfoot. We're going to scout the situation in San Antonio tonight. Then we'll know for sure what we're up against."

Seguin
September 1842

Jack Hays paced the floor of the temporary command post in the small community hall. He had done all he could now except wait.

The situation was as bad as Jack had feared. General Adrian Woll had firm control of San Antonio. Jack and Bigfoot Wallace had slipped to within spitting distance of Woll's forces and came away with an estimate of thirteen hundred troops. Jack was painfully satisfied with the accuracy of the estimate.

This time, Woll had taken prisoners, including the entire district court which had been in session on September 10. Every white male in San Antonio was now Woll's captive.

Jack had fifty-two men in his command at Seguin, counting the thirty-four Sam Walker had led back from San Antonio. But the messengers were out. Within the day, more Texans would be arriving, full of mad and ready to fight. "And this time, by God, we'll fight," Jack muttered to himself. "Enough is enough. If we have to attack them with six men, we'll do it."

Sam Walker stuck his head in the door. "Caldwell's here, Jack. Got eighty-five men with him. Never seen Old Paint this mad in my life."

Caldwell stormed into the room a few minutes later. Fury flashed in the old veteran's eyes. "What's the latest, Jack?" he asked abruptly. There was no time for the formality of greetings. "What's the battle plan?"

"I've got spies watching every move Woll makes," Jack said. "Antonio Perez will feed us information from inside San Antonio. In the meantime, we wait until more men get here. The rest, Colonel, is up to you. You're the ranking officer. I'm asking you to take command."

Old Paint Caldwell hesitated, rubbing a stubbled chin. "I don't know, Jack. Looks to me like you've got a pretty good handle on things."

"Colonel, I'm only a captain. There will be men riding into Seguin under the command of their own elected majors and colonels. Some of those officers might not take kindly to having a captain giving orders, and we don't have time to argue politics. Besides, a lot of those men served under you at Plum Creek and elsewhere. They trust your judgment." Jack reached for a spare cup and lifted the coffee pot from its rack on the fireplace. "I'm not trying to dodge responsibility. I'm just looking the duck in the quack."

Caldwell took the cup with a nod of thanks. "All right, Jack. You make sense. But if you have any ideas, squawk. I want to hear them."

Jack unfolded a map on the top of a bare table and touched a fingertip to a curve in a creek a few miles out of San Antonio. "We're going to be outgunned something fierce, Colonel. But if we can lure Woll to this bend in the Salado, we might gain an advantage.''

Caldwell glanced at the map and nodded. He knew the site well. "We'd have plenty of cover in the timber and brush. Woll would have to come at us over an open plain. We'd have three hundred yards with a good field of fire. With our best riflemen dug in the timber line, we could deal old Woll some pure misery, sure as badgers stink.''

Jack knew the old campaigner was thinking aloud as much as conducting a conversation.

"The trick is to get him there. Can your boys handle that, Jack?''

Jack glanced at Sam Walker. "Sam, what do you think?''

Walker grinned. "The general doesn't like Rangers, Jack. You and me in particular. He'd like nothing more than to wipe out the whole San Antonio company. He'll chase us anywhere we want him to.'' Walker glanced at Caldwell. "You just get your men there, Colonel. We'll bring you a whole passel of Mexicans to play with.''

Salado Creek
September 1842

Jack Hays winced as a rifle ball burned past his left ear and splatted into a tree trunk. General Adrian Woll had taken the bait. Now, Jack was beginning to wonder if the Texans had hooked a fish they couldn't land.

Woll had sent six hundred foot soldiers and two hundred cavalry in pursuit of Jack's Rangers. Now Woll had launched his attack. Mexican infantry poured onto the plain as cavalry units moved to the north to flank the Rangers, hoping to bury them in a cross fire. What the Mexican general didn't know was that more than Jack's small Ranger force waited in the timber. There were more than two hundred Texans waiting in ambush, dug into rifle pits and barricaded behind deadfalls of heavy tree trunks.

Matthew Caldwell stood beside a cottonwood tree, capped his

rifle and ignored the twigs which showered down on him as lead ripped through the branches above.

The advancing Mexican troops paused every fifty yards to kneel and fire toward the trees. Jack knew they were shooting blind. They couldn't find individual targets in the dense cover. The Texas sharpshooters held their fire, waiting for the Mexicans to close within sure target range.

Jack heard the crack of rifles to the rear as Woll's cavalry tried its flanking attack. He glanced over his shoulder toward the area where the creek twisted in an arc back toward the northeast. Heavy fire from the Gonzales volunteers hammered back the cavalry charge. Jack counted a dozen empty saddles as the Mexicans fell back.

"Pick your targets and give them hell, men!"

At Old Paint's yell, Texas rifles thundered. At least a dozen of Woll's infantry went down in the first volley. The Mexican charge stalled under the blistering fire from the timber, then collapsed as the foot soldiers fell back. The crack of Texas long rifles gradually faded as the Mexicans retreated beyond rifle range.

Jack glanced again over his shoulder. The cavalry unit that had tangled with the Gonzales volunteers milled about in confusion on open ground, apparently undecided whether to resume the attack or join the retreat. Jack waved toward his Ranger company waiting behind the rifle pits. "Mount up!" Jack called. He swung into the saddle and led his men from the brush in a headlong charge toward the Mexican cavalry. Texas battle cries ripped from thirty throats as the Rangers swept into the open, pistols in hand. The Mexican officer hesitated, surprised at the sudden charge of mounted men from the trees. Too late he realized they had him cut off from the main body of troops. He frantically tried to rally his men to face the charge. Jack felt Judas stumble and shudder as smoke billowed from a Mexican's pistol, but the sorrel kept his feet. Seconds later, the Rangers thundered into the cavalry ranks.

Jack slapped a shot, saw a rider sag in the saddle, thumbed the hammer of his revolver and fired again. A second man screamed and went down. The deadly crack of the Patersons ripped a hole in the loose formation of Mexican horsemen. The battle closed to individual combat, a swirl of powder smoke and dust.

Jack emptied his first pistol, thrust the weapon into his waistband, reached for the second handgun—and found himself staring into the big bore of a horse pistol in a Mexican's hand. He braced himself for the bullet shock. The Mexican suddenly toppled from the saddle, downed by a shot from a Ranger's weapon.

The swirling eye-to-eye battle ended as the surviving Mexicans rammed spurs to mounts, leaning low over their horses' necks in a desperate ride toward the main body of troops. Only six of them broke clear. One of the six had covered a hundred yards before Bigfoot Wallace's rifle put a ball between the man's shoulder blades. Ben McCulloch started to spur after the Mexicans, but checked his mount at Jack's yell: "Let 'em go, Ben! They've had enough!"

Jack broke both Patersons apart, dropped fresh cylinders into place and snapped the barrels home as he surveyed the battleground. Twelve Mexicans were down, dead or wounded. The Rangers had one man hurt, a powder burn across his neck and cheek. It looked worse than it was. Jack knew the man would carry a peppery blue-black brand on his face for the rest of his life. But he would live.

"Well, Captain, we kicked some Mexican butts out here." Jack glanced at Bill Davis. The big Ranger's grin was a white slash through the grime of battle.

"Yes, I guess we did," Jack said. "But there's plenty more—" A shudder between his knees broke Jack's words. Judas staggered. Jack kicked free of the stirrups and landed on his feet as the sorrel went down. Jack watched, uncomprehending for a moment. Then he remembered the sorrel's stumble during the charge.

A red stain spread across Judas's ribs behind the saddle cinch. Pink bubbles frothed at the edge of the bit in the horse's mouth. Bill Davis knelt at the animal's side, then looked up and shook his head. "Sorry, Jack. He's gutshot. We can't save him."

Jack fought back a sudden wave of nausea. "Dammit, Judas," he said softly to the horse, "this was going to be your last patrol." He raised his revolver. A strong hand settled over Jack's wrist, pushing the gun aside. "I'll do it, Jack," Davis said.

Jack swallowed and nodded, not trusting himself to speak. He turned his back. The crack of Bill Davis's pistol cut an icy track through Jack's belly. He felt a hand on his shoulder.

"Old Judas went like a Ranger ought to go, Jack. In battle," Bigfoot Wallace said. "Ben's horse will ride double. I'll bring your saddle and other stuff."

The Battle of the Salado settled into a grim, bloody routine. The Texans repulsed charge after charge, leaving the plain littered with crumpled, uniformed bodies. Jack, mounted now on a strong, solid bay whose owner would never need it again, led his Ranger company from the timber to slash into foraging or scouting parties, to tease a platoon or more into pursuit and into an ambush, or to suddenly wheel in full stride to attack the pursuers. And always nipping at the flanks of the enemy.

During a lull in the battle Jack heard the distant *thump* of the Mexican cannon firing as rapidly as gunners could load. He was about to ride out to investigate when the battle on the creek again turned heated.

At nightfall the firing stopped on both sides of the plain. The two armies turned to treating their wounded, burying their dead and checking supplies.

Jack finished cleaning and reloading his second pistol and went in search of Old Paint Caldwell. He found the colonel leaning against the bole of a pecan tree, swearing bitterly. Rage and pain twisted Old Paint's face. "What happened, Colonel?" Jack asked.

"Damn Mexican cannon," Caldwell snapped. "They caught Nicholas Dawson and fifty men riding in from LaGrange. Stayed out of rifle range and cut them up with cannon fire." Caldwell swallowed hard. "Dawson tried to surrender. Damn Mexicans ignored the white flag, just kept pounding away at them. No more than ten or eleven of the LaGrange boys got away and most of them were wounded."

Caldwell glared toward the fires of the Mexican Army camp in the distance. "Dammit," he said, "Nicholas Dawson never knew how to fight Mexicans. But by God, Jack, *we* know how—and I'll have that bastard Woll's *cojones* for supper tomorrow or know the reason why!"

· · · ·

By sunrise the next day, General Adrian Woll had had enough. The Mexicans began to withdraw, leaving behind those too badly wounded to travel. Caldwell's force had grown by another hundred men during the night. Old Paint placed fifteen more seasoned veterans under Jack's command. "Give 'em hell, son," was Caldwell's only instruction.

Jack's Rangers carved away at the Mexican troops. They slashed through foraging parties, wiped out a cavalry patrol that wandered too far from Woll's main body of troops and lured an entire company of less wary dragoons into an ambush. A trail of Mexican bodies marked Woll's retreat.

Near the San Antonio Road crossing, Woll's rear guard wheeled the cannon to the top of a low rise facing the Texas lines, with half a hundred infantrymen to protect the field piece. The cannon's thunder did little damage, but it did slow the dogged pursuit of the Texans.

"Those bastards on that cannon are the ones that wiped out Dawson's command," Old Paint snapped. "I'm going to make 'em pay for that—I'll take that gun, stick it up Woll's ass and let fly a couple of canister rounds."

"Let my Rangers take care of it, Colonel," Jack said. He heard the hard edge in his own voice. "No sense risking an infantry attack. We'll get the piece for you."

A quarter hour later, Jack led thirty Rangers into a skirmish line in full view of the cannoneers. He could see the Mexicans frantically trying to bring the piece to bear on the men who had suddenly appeared at their flank. Jack held a hand aloft. Thad Green kneed his horse alongside Jack's bay as the Rangers pulled their mounts to a halt, awaiting Jack's command. "Think it'll work, Captain?"

"It'll work, Thad. We give them sixty seconds, then charge. Mexican gunners always overshoot on the first round. We'll be on them before they can reload. They won't get much help from the infantry. Those boys are just a touch afraid of us, I think." He stared toward the cannon for a few more seconds, then swept his hand forward and yelled, "Charge!"

The cannon boomed, but as Jack had predicted, the round went high. The Rangers thundered up the rise. A dozen or so Mexican infantrymen fired, also overshooting the target in their haste; the rest threw down their guns and ran, the Texas yell spurring them on. Jack reined the bay toward the cannon's off-wheel and fired his revolver into the back of an artilleryman who was trying to ram a canister charge down the barrel. The Texans swarmed over the gun crew and remaining infantrymen. It was more of a slaughter than a fight. Close-range shotgun and pistol work was a Ranger specialty. Not a Mexican was left alive at the cannon. Three survived the initial charge; Bowie knives silenced quickly their pleas for mercy.

Matthew Caldwell himself took control of the field piece, sending round after round to burst amid Woll's rear guard, smashing supply wagons, stampeding horses and scattering infantrymen. Texas riflemen thinned ranks scattered by the cannon. By sunset Woll's troops were fighting for their lives; Ben McCulloch and Bigfoot Wallace slipped into the Mexican camp under the cover of darkness. At dawn the next day, the severed heads of four soldiers greeted Woll when he emerged from his tent.

Four days later, the battered Mexican force sloshed across the Rio Grande as the catcalls and whoops of the Texans rang over the muddy water.

The invasion of Texas was over.

Bigfoot Wallace leaned from the saddle and scooped a piece of paper from the water's edge. He read the printed sheet slowly and ponderously. A wide grin spread over the frontiersman's face.

"Well, Captain," he said to Jack, "it looks like you've done become a man of some value after all." He handed over a scrap of paper. "Little keepsake for you. General Adrian Woll has gone and put a reward of five hundred dollars in silver on your head." Wallace chuckled aloud. "Seems a plumb high price for a hundred-sixty-pound man who ain't seen his twenty-sixth birthday yet."

TEN

San Antonio
October 1842

Jack Hays leaned against the rough plank wall of the box stall
and let his body unwind after yet another long patrol along the
Nueces and the desert beyond. The sound of the bay crunching
grain helped ease the nerves. The bay was a compact, powerful
horse, worth at least the hundred dollars Jack had sent to the
family of the man killed at Salado Creek. The animal was alert
and responsive to the touch, light on his feet during battle, gentle and eager to please his rider.

Jack still missed Judas. He and the unpredictable sorrel had
been through too much together. Judas almost always pitched
on cold mornings, and sometimes even after a hard day's ride
under a broiling sun. He had been hell's own handful when it
came time to replace worn-out horseshoes, and he had put many
a bruise on Jack during those farrier sessions. But battles shared
and miles traveled formed bonds between horse and rider as well
as between men.

He forced the thoughts of Judas from his mind. What was
done stayed done. Nothing could change that, and there were
other things to worry about.

The patrols since Woll's defeat had found no sign of another
Mexican invasion force. The Mexican Army had retreated beyond the Rio Grande, and appeared disinclined to return. Nor

had the patrols cut sign of any Indian war parties. Not a single Comanche depredation had been reported since the Salado fight. The frontier was quiet. Jack had learned long ago that the time to get cautious, if not downright nervous, was when things were quiet.

It wasn't quiet on the streets of San Antonio. Most of the solid, dependable volunteers had gone home after chasing Woll over the Rio Grande. But scores of the Salado Creek force had stayed in San Antonio, and most of them were the less desirable types. The saloons and cantinas did a land office business, fights were more common than flies and the whores now had more money than the legitimate merchants.

So far, no one had been killed. Jack wondered how long that stretch of luck would ride. He walked back to his office, settled into the chair behind his cluttered desk and tried to put himself in Sam Houston's boots.

The political scene these days was as noisy as the streets of San Antonio, Jack reflected. The howl of outrage that followed the Vasquez foray into Texas was a whimper in a whirlwind compared to the public reaction to the Woll invasion. Texans and non-Texans alike clamored for a declaration of war against Mexico. Support for such an action had spread beyond Texas borders, even across the seas to Europe. In the United States Congress, the proposal to annex Texas—or at least to grant territorial status—was steadily gaining supporters. The political pressure on Houston had to be enormous, Jack knew. No man could tolerate the wrath of the people for long and expect to remain in elective office.

A hammering on the door interrupted Jack's musings. A man in the uniform of a militia general, his tunic and cap heavy with brass and braid, stood in the doorway. "You must be Captain Jack Hays of the Texas Rangers," the officer said.

"I am."

Brass-and-braid stripped off a gauntlet and offered a hand to Jack. "Brigadier General Alexander Somervell." Jack took the hand. The general's grip was on the limp side, the hands smooth, uncallused and damp. Somervell's ruddy face was flushed. There was a weakness about the jaw and eyes that Jack didn't like.

"Something I can do for you, General?" Jack motioned toward a chair. It was the most uncomfortable one in the place. Somervell sat heavily and sighed. "A long and dusty road, Captain." It was a hint as much as a travel report.

"Sorry I haven't anything stronger than water to offer, General. Care for a dipper?"

Somervell's jowls sagged in disappointment. "I thought all you frontier types were hard drinkers."

Jack shrugged. "Some are. But my men don't drink on duty, which is most of the time, and I don't keep a bottle in the office. I can send for one, if you wish."

Somervell shook his head. "Later, perhaps. We have business to discuss, Captain." The general pulled folded papers from the pocket of his tunic. "I have been instructed by President Houston to organize a force to invade Mexico."

Jack tried not to show his surprise.

"Provided," Somervell continued, "that in my opinion it can be done successfully. The President wishes you to assist me."

"Excuse me, General," Jack said. "You said *organize* a force? Am I to understand you currently have no troops under your command?"

Somervell waved the paper toward the door. "This is to be strictly a volunteer effort, Captain. I have about four hundred men on the way, a few militia veterans and some East Texas ranging companies. I plan to raise another three hundred—including your frontier Rangers, of course—here in San Antonio. And your counterpart, Ranger Captain Ewen Cameron, is on his way from Lavaca with eighty or so men."

Jack fell silent for a moment, wondering if the entire idea were some kind of joke. Or if Houston had gone mad.

"General, I'm not sure we can raise even a hundred good men for such a venture—"

"Nonsense, Captain," Somervell interrupted, "there are plenty of able-bodied men in your city." Somervell unfolded the papers in his hand. "Here, Captain Hays. Let me read you a passage from my orders, in President Houston's own handwriting." The general cleared his throat. "Ah, yes, here it is: 'You may rely upon the gallant Hays and his companions; and I desire that you obtain his services and co-operation, and assure him and all the brave and subordinate men in the field, that the hopes of the country and the confidence of the Executive point to them as objects of constant solicitude.' " Somervell handed the papers to Jack. "You may wish to verify the contents, Captain."

Jack glanced at the general's orders. They were in Sam Houston's handwriting. Jack knew the flowing penmanship and the President's signature well. Messages from the capital, often from Houston himself, arrived almost daily at Jack's headquarters. Jack handed the papers back to Somervell, who refolded them and returned them to his pocket.

"So there you have it, Captain Hays," the general said. "President Houston personally has asked you to serve as my subordinate for the invasion of Mexico."

Jack leaned against the desk, trying to organize his thoughts. The whole concept was ludicrous. *So Houston finally gave in to the pressure to do something,* Jack thought bitterly. *He's handing out a sop to public opinion. With us as target practice for Mexican troops.*

"Well, Captain?"

Jack pushed himself away from the desk. "May I be perfectly honest with you, General?"

Somervell nodded. "Of course." Jack saw the sudden flare of suspicion in the general's eyes.

"With all due respect, sir, I have grave reservations about such a plan. The East Texas Rangers and the militia are woodsmen, accustomed to fighting afoot and in the forests. This will be a desert campaign fought on enemy soil. It should be executed by cavalry forces to have a chance of success. The East Texans are undeniably brave men, but they have no experience in fighting Mexicans. Most of the men now in San Antonio are drifters and freebooters, more interested in loot than in a cause. In a word, sir, they're rabble. I wouldn't trust them in a fight."

Somervell's ruddy face drew into a scowl. "Captain Hays, are you questioning President Houston's judgment?"

"In this particular campaign, yes. That said, however, I add that I have no choice but to follow the President's orders to the best of my ability."

Somervell heaved himself erect and glowered at Jack. "Captain Hays, I trust this reluctance of yours will not be an impediment on the field of battle."

Jack leveled a steady, cold glare at Somervell. "General, do not confuse an observation of reality with reluctance. The Texas Rangers will fight."

Somervell's challenge wilted under Jack's gaze. "Very well, Captain Hays. We start recruiting immediately. I expect your Rangers to be among the first to assemble."

Somervell did not offer a hand as he left, and Jack wasn't sure he would have taken it if offered. Not after an insult like that. Jack forced away his anger. There was too much to be done to broil a gut over a personal fire.

Guerrero, Mexico
December 1842

Captain Jack Hays squatted beside a small, smoky greasewood fire at the edge of the Somervell invasion force's camp and struggled to control his disgust. He had never seen a campaign so badly botched.

Somervell had proven to be an even more inept leader than Jack had feared. The general had ignored Jack's advice at every turn. And now he had lost control of his army.

Somervell's own officers had grown disgusted with their commander. Discipline in the ranks, shaky to begin with, had totally disintegrated at Laredo. Somervell's troops had gone on a rampage. The town now was little more than rubble. Soldiers looted homes, leaving the already poor peons with nothing, not even food for their families. Women had been abused and raped. Then, when Somervell finally tried to restore a semblance of order and demanded the arrest of a handful of the worst outlaws in the ranks, two hundred men had walked out of camp.

The initial invasion force of seven hundred fifty now stood at less than five hundred. To those who remained it had become increasingly clear that Somervell did not have the will to engage the Mexican Army. Now Somervell had decided to abandon the campaign entirely and ordered a withdrawal to Texas soil. That, Jack grumbled to himself, was the first logical move the general had made.

Jack stood as Sam Walker, Bigfoot Wallace and Ewen Cameron strode into the circle of weak light cast by the camp fire.

"Jack, we need to talk." Sam's voice was tight, his eyes narrowed to slits, jaw and shoulders squared. Jack knew the signs well. Sam Walker was mad to the bone. Jack glanced at the other two men. Bigfoot's jaws worked a chew with an intensity seldom seen in the broad, generally placid face. Cameron's shoulders were hunched forward; the big Scot's expression reminded Jack of a thundercloud looking for some place to put a lightning bolt.

"What's on your mind, men?" Jack asked.

"This whole campaign, Jack." Walker's mouth twisted in disgust. "It's been a damn mess from day one. Some of us have decided to do something about it."

Jack raised an eyebrow.

"Captain Hays," Ewen Cameron said, "we've been talking it over. There are a lot of us who intend to see this invasion through. We aren't going back. We're going on to Mexico City."

"Damn whistlin' we are." Bigfoot Wallace spat into the fire. "Sam Houston wants an invasion and a war with Mexico, by damn he'll get one. Jack, I come to Texas to kill Mexicans, like they killed my kin. I ain't done yet."

"We figure we can raise three hundred reliable men out of this bunch," Cameron said. "Colonel Fisher and his men are willing and eager. We can't let it stop here."

Jack turned to Sam Walker and frowned in disapproval. "Sam, by now half of the Mexican Army will be on its way here. I'm not sure this is a good idea."

"Good or not, Jack, we're going. We want you to come with us."

Jack shook his head. "I'm here on Houston's orders. I'll obey them." He saw the disappointment flare in Sam's face. For a moment Jack considered ordering all the Rangers in his command back to San Antonio. At the same moment he realized it would accomplish nothing. A man led Rangers. He didn't order them around like they were schoolboys. "I'll not stand in your way if you've made your decision." Jack kept his voice firm and level with an effort. "All I can do is advise you to reconsider. I've ridden some long trails with you. I'd hate to lose some more friends, and you know the odds you'll be facing."

"Odds never stopped a real Texan before, Jack," Sam Walker said. "They sure as hell never stopped a Ranger."

Jack sighed. There was nothing more he could do. No amount of debate, reasoned or otherwise, would change these men's minds once they were made up. "Then all I can do is wish you well—and ask you to keep your heads down when the shooting gets heavy."

Jack Hays twisted in the saddle for a last look back at the Guerrero campsite, an empty feeling in his gut.

Ben McCulloch rode at Jack's side. "Think we'll ever see them again, Jack?"

Jack turned back, facing straight ahead. Almost half his own company had stayed behind—Wallace, Walker, Bill Davis, a dozen other good men. "I don't know, Ben. All we can do now is wait. And hope—"

San Antonio
April 1843

Jack Hays led his weary patrol of eight men through the quagmire of the streets of San Antonio. The driving rain hammered at the Rangers' gum coats, sent rivulets trickling down saddle-stiff backs and poured in steady streams from hat brims. Lightning danced from the clouds overhead, each jagged bolt touching off the boom of nature's artillery.

Jack waved the patrol to a halt, dismissed the men with his thanks for their efforts and reined the bay toward the stable. The black sky overhead matched his own bleak mood.

The Texas campaign into Mexico had been a disaster.

Three hundred men, including many of his friends and fellow Rangers, had set out from Guerrero. Less than a hundred seventy survived what had become known as the Mier Expedition, named for the town where they were captured after a bitter,

bloody battle against General Pedro de Ampudia's thousand-
plus Mexican troops.

From official reports, newspaper accounts and messages from
his many contacts, Jack knew the sequence of events as well as if
he had been at Mier himself. Ampudia had promised the Mier
captives would be treated as prisoners of war, and would be held
near the Texas border. But the hated Antonio Canales out-
ranked Ampudia; he had marched the men deep into the interior of Mexico. At Hacienda Salado, Ewen Cameron and Sam
Walker led an escape that ended in failure in the barren desert
waste between Saltillo and the Rio Grande. Only five men made
it back to Texas. Santa Anna flew into a murderous rage over the
escape and ordered the execution of all the Mier survivors. Only
intense pressure from American and British diplomats had saved
the men from the firing squad—most of them, anyway.

Santa Anna, in a sudden burst of generosity, offered a compromise. He ordered death by lottery for every tenth man. Seventeen black beans and one hundred fifty-nine white ones were put
into a jar; Texans who drew black beans were lined up against an
adobe wall and shot. Ewen Cameron drew a white bean. It
hadn't saved him. Canales hated Cameron worse than he hated
other Texans. The Scot, who twice had defeated Canales in
clashes along the border, was led to the wall and cut down by a
Mexican firing squad. Those who survived now were in the
prison at Perote, the most notorious hellhole of Mexican pris-
ons. Jack wondered how many Texans would survive Perote.

Jack stripped the saddle from the bay and tended the horse,
his movements mechanical, his mind with the men at Perote. He
sloshed through the mud to his office. Ben McCulloch was waiting.

"No luck with the Comanche raiders, Jack?"

Jack shook the water from his coat and hat and hung them on
pegs to dry. "No, Ben. We never even got within a day's ride.
This damned rain—" His voice trailed away.

Ben waited patiently as Jack stripped, toweled dry and dressed
in fresh clothes. A cup of coffee was waiting on Jack's desk when
he stepped back into the office.

"I just got back from Austin this morning, Jack. All hell's
breaking loose over the Mier thing."

"Any news on who's still alive?" Jack sipped at the coffee, let the hot liquid drive the chill from his belly and settled into a chair to stretch the saddle ache from his knees.

"Sam made it. So did Bigfoot and Bill Davis. Not sure yet about the others." Ben lifted another cup from the mantel rack and filled it, then puffed across the dark liquid to cool it. "Jack, it's a hell of a thing to think about. But it looks like the Mier thing will have some good to it after all. Old Santa Anna has shot himself in the foot this time. He's catching hell from everybody, including some of his own people, over the black bean affair. Newspapers back East are full of the 'atrocity,' as they call it." Ben grimaced. "They don't understand it's just the Mexican way of doing business." Ben paused as a powerful boom of thunder rattled the shutters covering the windows. Then the hint of a smile touched his lips. "Jack, it looks like we're going to get them back."

"What?"

"Word in Austin is that Santa Anna's agreed to release our men at Perote, along with some other Texans he's got."

"When?"

Ben shrugged. "Don't know. We still haven't heard mention of any specific day. Santa Anna's trying to find a way to save face, to uphold Mexican 'honor'—as if they had any." Ben tapped a finger against his coffee cup. "Word also is that Santa Anna's going to offer Texas a peace treaty. And that Houston's going to step around the offer."

"Why would he—wait a minute!" Jack almost lunged out of the chair. "Ben, I've been thinking Sam Houston's lost his mind. But I think I see now what he's doing—he's working this like a poker game and he's holding aces. What Houston wants is full statehood for Texas. And the old fox may just get it." Jack paced as he talked, his exhaustion chased by the sudden understanding. "If Houston accepts a peace treaty, it eases the pressure on Congress to annex Texas. If he ducks it, it just tightens the thumbscrews." Jack stopped pacing and grinned at Ben McCulloch. "It looks like I owe Houston an apology."

Ben chuckled. "Jack, I'm beginning to get worried about you. You're starting to think like a politician."

ELEVEN

San Antonio
October 1843

Jack Hays scanned the last of the official reports and personal letters that had accumulated during his twelve-day patrol along the Llano and Sabinal rivers. He pushed the documents aside, realizing he had greatly underestimated the role of Texas in national and world politics.

Jack wasn't surprised that Sam Houston had ducked Mexico's offer of a formal peace treaty and, instead, declared a truce. That had been four months ago. So far Mexico had observed the cease-fire.

The Comanches hadn't been nearly as cooperative. Technically, Houston's peace treaty with the Southern Plains tribes remained in effect. But when the Somervell debacle and the Mier Expedition drained so many good men from Ranger ranks, the Paneteka mounted a series of quick, slashing raids. Sometimes Jack's luck held; more often the Indians escaped, occasionally with a white captive to go along with horses and mules stolen in the summer and fall raids.

Indian troubles aside, Texas was gaining ground. President Tyler had finally bitten the bullet and offered annexation to Texas as a territory. Jack doubted Houston would go for it. Designation as a territory and not a state was half an apple. It would leave Texas responsible for its own defense, without sufficient financial backing, or even voting representation in the U.S. Congress. Houston wanted the whole thing. Full statehood. *It'll be interesting to see how old Sam handles this one,* Jack thought.

He glanced up as Ben McCulloch stepped into the room. A smile played across Ben's normally serious face. "We drew a pair of good news aces for a change, Jack," he said. "Word just came in by courier—Santa Anna's turning our Mier people loose."

Jack felt a surge of relief. "They're coming home?"

Ben nodded. "That's the first good news card. The second is that the Walker Colts are here. Teamster's on his way with them. Be here any minute now. Damn me if this isn't better than Christmas."

An hour later Jack sat at his desk, a wooden box before him. His name was engraved on a silver plate set into the wood. He lifted the lid. Two of the big Walker Colts rested in the case along with powder flask, cap box and tools. A note lay faceup: "For Texas Ranger Captain Jack Hays, compliments of Samuel Colt."

"My God, Jack—did you ever see such a work in your life?" Ben McCulloch held a similar box in his lap. His words held more than a touch of awe.

Jack lifted one of the weapons from the presentation case. He estimated its weight at better than four and a half pounds, but it settled solid and smooth to the hand. The balance was almost perfect. The weapon was forty-four caliber, a man-stopper, with a nine-inch octagonal barrel and a rammer lever under the barrel for reloading. It had six chambers, a blade front sight and a notch cut into the hammer to serve as a rear sight when the weapon was cocked. The trigger, with a square-backed brass guard, was fixed and visible—not the parlor-trick disappearing trigger of the Paterson. "Ben, this is a Ranger's gun." Jack heard the reverence in his own words, like a preacher opening a wedding ceremony.

"Take a look at the cylinder, Jack. That's you in the engraving. With a Paterson, in the Nueces Canyon fight."

Jack studied the fine lines etched on the cylinder. The stylized scene depicted a Ranger with pistol in hand charging a group of Indians. "Well, I'll be damned," Jack muttered.

Ben cocked an eyebrow at Jack. "It's still light enough to see if they'll shoot."

They would.

Jack shook his head in amazement as he examined his target. Four of his last six shots had hit within the span of a man's hand at twenty paces. The splintered pine board used as a target was ample testimony to the power of the forty-four-caliber slug. The substantial weight of the weapon damped the recoil; the gun kicked less than Jack had expected from a big-bore pistol carrying a heavy powder charge. The heft and solid construction also made the gun a sturdy club if a man should be caught with an empty chamber in close quarters, or facing someone who "wasn't worth shooting," as Sam Walker had said after his trip back East to help design his namesake.

Ben McCulloch's target groups were consistently smaller than Jack's, but Jack conceded Ben was more of a *pistolero* to begin with.

Sundown brought an end to the practice session. The two Rangers returned to the office, and stripped and cleaned the Walkers by lamplight. *The accumulation of black powder residue would have choked a Paterson down,* Jack thought as he swabbed at the chambers of the Walker, but the new Colts had not malfunctioned a single time.

"Jack, there's another cased set here," Ben said solemnly. "It's got Sam's name on it."

"We'll save it for him. A welcome home present for when he gets back."

San Antonio
September 1844

The return of the Mier Expedition captives triggered mixed emotions on the Texas frontier.

The first was joy at the return of the survivors. That soon turned to outrage as their first-hand accounts became known. The brutality, hardship and starvation endured by those who lived stirred new hatred for Mexico among the Texans. Personal accounts of the "black bean" death lottery fueled the fury that had swept the Republic and the American nation when the news first spread beyond Mexico.

Jack Hays shared the bitter rage of the Mier men as he listened to the stories and read the accounts. No man had smiled or cheered when he drew a white bean, for that meant sure death awaited a companion who had not yet reached into the bean jar. Those who drew black beans accepted their fate and went before the Mexican firing squad in composed defiance. There were tears on the faces of some of the Mexican soldiers detailed to carry out the executions, but none of the Texans had wept or cursed his luck.

Accounts of deprivation, beatings and forced slave labor wove a common thread through the tapestry of stories told by the Mier survivors.

Not all the tales were grim. Several men recalled how Bigfoot Wallace, harnessed to pull a heavy cart loaded with building materials, whooped and staged a "runaway," scattering rocks, dirt, pieces of the cart and startled Mexicans as he charged through the streets. "Old Bigfoot made a damn poor work mule," Bill Davis said with a grin and a shake of the head, "and they couldn't even get his attention with a two-by-four between the ears."

Sam Walker, Jack noted, seldom spoke of his days in captivity. "I buried a dime under the flagpole at Perote," he said, "and, by God, one day I'll go back and dig it up." After that declaration he was silent on the matter, but Jack noticed a new and hard look in Sam's eye when a strange Mexican came near. Several times, Jack had observed Sam sitting in a cane chair in front of the Ranger office or in the saddle atop a small rise, hand resting on one of his new Walker Colts, as he stared toward the south, jaw set and square. *There's going to be hell to pay,* Jack thought, *when this bunch rides back into Mexico—and they will. It's the nature of the animal.*

Most of the captives, all strong men to begin with, quickly regained their health with adequate food, medical care and rest. A few were physically broken by the experience, their bodies unable to repair the damage.

Jack kept his men as busy as their physical condition allowed.

The Comanches wound up paying the price. Jack and thirteen Rangers, each armed with a pair of the new Colts, caught up with one band of forty raiders along the Pedernales River. The Rangers fought with the fury of madmen; at the end of the initial pitched battle and running fight that followed, only fifteen Indians escaped. The patrol brought back two white captives and recovered thirty stolen horses. The Pedernales fight was only one of a half-dozen skirmishes, but it had been the battle that brought a heightened fear of the Rangers to the Comanches. Indian raids into the wide region patrolled by the San Antonio Ranger company dropped to little more than harassment or horse stealing raids by small bands of the more foolish young warriors.

Jack made it a point not to take the Mier Expedition survivors on patrols along the Nueces and into the Mustang Desert beyond. It was too soon to bring the Mier men into contact with Mexican troops. Occasionally, Rangers on patrol along the border found themselves facing a Mexican patrol across the disputed boundary line. Jack wasn't sure he could stop Wallace, Walker and Davis from charging an entire Mexican regiment, should one appear. So he didn't take the chance.

For now, all was quiet on the border. There had been no signs of any significant troop movements or buildup in northern Mexico. That was something of a surprise to Jack, given the rapid developments on the political front over the past year. In June, the United States Senate had blocked the annexation of Texas as a territory. Now the Texas question had become a powerful issue in the U.S. presidential race. A compromise candidate, James Knox Polk, was chosen in the wake of a rift between pro-annexation and anti-annexation Democrats.

Jack sensed the hand of Sam Houston at work in both instances. The senators who blocked the territorial annexation plan were an odd combination of anti-slavery men and Southerners who now were committed to full statehood for Texas. In the second instance, Polk was a personal friend of Houston, and shared the expansionist dreams of both Houston and Andrew Jackson. And the Democrats had managed to tie the Texas issue to Oregon, where New Englanders by the hundreds were settling. Polk's campaign war cry, "Reoccupation of Oregon and reannexation of Texas,'' condensed to "Fifty-four forty or fight" for popular consumption, had finally pushed the American people into embracing the importance of Texas in the national dream of expansion. It also was straining relations with the British, who had claims to Oregon and were now actively courting Texas as a possible power base to regain leverage previously lost to the United States of America.

Jack had expected the Mexicans to heat up to full boil and pour across the river in force. Since they hadn't, this would be a good time to call on Susan Calvert. She had been living in Seguin for more than a month now. He retrieved a package from his living quarters and strode toward the stable, remembering the parting words of the silversmith who had crafted the silver tray in the package: "I think this one you will marry, Captain Jack. She must be a very special woman."

"Yes," Jack muttered aloud as he saddled the bay, "she is a very special woman."

Seguin
October 1844

Jack Hays reined his horse up to the hitch rail before the new home on the outskirts of Seguin. His palms were sweaty despite the mild day and the cool breeze from the north, and he could feel the pound of his heart against his ribs. *Jack Hays, Texas Ranger,* he scolded himself, *who can ride into a Comanche camp or a Mexican Army without blinking, afraid of facing a hundred-ten-pound woman.*

The door swung open and Susan Calvert stepped onto the porch. The wind rustled her hair, which tumbled free around her shoulders. *My God, she's even more beautiful than I remembered,* Jack thought.

Susan was at his side by the time he had stepped down from the big bay. "Jack, it's so good to see you again," she said. She offered a slender hand. "I was so afraid you wouldn't be able to visit. I know you stay awfully busy."

"Not so busy that I couldn't bring you a housewarming gift,

Susan," Jack said as he pulled the package from a saddlebag. "And to welcome you as a neighbor. Seguin isn't really all that far from San Antonio, at least not by Texas standards."

She took the package in one hand and tucked the other beneath his upper arm. "Thank you so much, Jack. Come inside, meet the family, have some coffee and let me see what treasure you have brought. Then, if you aren't too tired, would you go riding with me? There's so much of the country here I've yet to see."

Jack liked the feel of the long-legged Tennessee black between his knees. The horse had a presence, the sense that the powerful muscles were under strict control, and he was quick to respond to the bit or to the pressure of the knees.

Jack was surprised to learn that Susan had broken and trained the black herself. "Sometimes I don't quite fit the mold of the domestic female, Jack," she said. "I hope you don't hold that against me."

He didn't. It was just one more thing to admire about her. "What's his name?"

"Justin," Susan said.

"Strange name for a horse."

"When he was foaled, father wasn't impressed with his looks," Susan said with a smile. "Father said he was just another horse. So that's the name I gave him—Justin Otherhorse."

Jack chuckled aloud. "He's anything but just another horse. Would you consider selling him?"

Susan shook her head. "Justin isn't for sale, Jack. He's rather special to me."

They rode in silence for a time before pulling the horses to a stop at the edge of a stand of pecan and oak trees on the sunny downwind slope of a grassy hill. They dismounted, enjoying the view of rolling hills, timber and meadows.

"It's such a beautiful country, Jack," Susan said, her voice soft. "There's—I don't know how to explain it—a majesty about it, a sense of freedom. It's as if God built Texas with a specific plan in mind. Or maybe He was just showing off His powers a bit."

Jack found no quarrel with that observation.

They stood for a long time side by side. Jack grew increasingly conscious of her scent, a delicate combination of lilac water, horse and leather.

"Jack," Susan finally said, "what will you do when war with Mexico comes?"

"Whatever is asked of me. I can't do less."

"And when it's over? Will you leave the Rangers?"

Jack sighed. "I haven't had time to give that much thought. I'll have to resign from the Rangers, of course. That's a young man's calling, and one without much of a future. I suppose I'll return to my old trade. There's a lot of country yet to be surveyed."

"Will you be happy at that, Jack? It seems—well, rather tame compared to what your life has been out here."

"I suppose it would depend on the circumstances," he said.

"Yes, I guess it would at that." Susan turned to face Jack. There seemed to be a hint of moisture at the corners of her eyes. She came into his arms, kissed him, then buried her face into the spot where his neck and shoulder joined. "God," she said, "what a forward woman I am. You must think I'm a slut."

"Susan, that's the last thing I would ever think."

"Then we'd better start back before I do something to make you think so, Jack Hays." She snuggled against him for a moment longer, then eased from his embrace. "When will I see you again?"

Jack smiled at her. "Every time I get the chance and until you tell me to stay away, Susan Calvert."

TWELVE

Medina River
April 1845

Jack Hays ignored the deerflies buzzing around his neck and face as he led his ten-man patrol along the bank of the sluggish stream, near the end of a week-long patrol that had taken them from the bend of the Nueces into the Hill Country.

They had found no sign of Comanches or of Mexican troops. Now, saddle-weary and short of rations, they were heading home. For the last five miles the men had ridden in silence. A Ranger spent a great deal of his life in the boredom of riding through empty country, searching for signs of someone or something who wasn't there. They learned to tolerate the boredom, but they never learned to like it.

At Jack's side, Bill Davis suddenly reined in his horse and gestured toward the stagnant green water of a slough at a bend in the Medina River. Jack followed the line pointed out by Davis's finger. The nostrils and bulging eye sockets of a large alligator protruded above the scum. Davis dismounted, stripped off his gunbelt and shirt.

"What the devil are you up to now, Bill?" Jack asked.

Davis grinned up at Jack. "We're always short-handed, Captain. I'm going to muster that critter into the company." Before Jack could protest, Davis had plunged into the slough.

"That damn fool is going to get himself killed," Thad Green said, reaching for his rifle.

Jack raised a hand. "Hold off a minute, Thad. Bill just needs to work off a little aggravation." *What the hell; we all do,* he thought. "Besides, I'm a touch curious how this might turn out. I'll put four bits on Bill Davis."

"Cover that bet," Thad said. "That 'gator is a good six foot long."

The thick water boiled as Ranger and alligator collided. Both disappeared from sight for a moment, then surfaced; Bill Davis had a half nelson on the alligator's neck with his right arm, his left hand reaching for the snout at the end of the powerful jaws. The alligator broke free with a violent twist, snapped at Davis, missed, then whirled and slashed with a heavy tail. Jack heard Davis grunt as the tail slammed into his side. Then man and beast again disappeared beneath the roiling, greasy water.

The struggle went on for better than fifteen minutes before Bill Davis, his body covered with mud, welts and scratches, wrestled the alligator onto the creek bank. He had the animal's snout clamped in a big hand as he plopped down astride the alligator's neck. "Swear the bastard in, Jack," Davis said, breathing hard.

Jack solemnly recited the Ranger oath. Davis pumped the alligator's head up and down in a nodding motion. "He's took the oath. He's a private in Company C now, Captain." Davis released the alligator and jumped free just before sharp, jagged teeth snapped near his heel. The alligator scurried toward the safety of the water.

Bill Davis sat erect, chest heaving. A wide grin spread over his muddy face. "Damn tough 'gator," he said. "Make a helluva Ranger." Davis probed his side with a hand. "Private Al E. Gator over there near busted a rib for me."

Thad Green shook his head in mock disgust, fished in a pocket and handed a coin to Jack. Jack dropped the money into his shirt pocket, retrieved his notebook and made a note that Company C had a new recruit—unpaid, of course—and the date. He closed the book and grinned at Davis.

"Feel better now, Bill?"

"Yeah. Lots better." Davis reached for his shirt and winced. "Good scrap. Thought old Alley had me there a couple times."

Thad Green snorted. "Better mount up, Alligator," he said. "We might run across a catamount on the way home. Want you rested for that."

Jack waited until Davis had remounted, then kneed his bay toward San Antonio. He knew that from this day on, Bill Davis had a nickname. Alligator Davis. Kind of had a ring to it, Jack thought—at least for a big Texas Ranger.

San Antonio
October 1845

Jack Hays signed the final copy of the official report and closed the Company C record book. The reorganization of the Texas Rangers was now complete.

He was now Major John Coffee Hays, officially in command of three separate Ranger companies—his own and two new units, one commanded by Sam Walker, the other by Ben McCulloch, each with the rank of captain.

Technically, the Ranger force had been expanded to provide more protection for the Texas frontier. Jack suspected the real reason was that General Zachary Taylor wanted a cavalry force handy. Taylor's American Army troops, already in position in Corpus Christi on the Texas coast, were all dragoon or infantry units. He had no one who knew the country south and west of the Nueces, no cavalry to scout enemy movements and find routes with sufficient water to support an army on the march, no mounted men to oppose Mexican horse soldiers. It was obvious to anyone past the age of six that Taylor would need the Rangers, Jack thought.

The annexation of Texas was only a matter of weeks, a few months at the outside, from becoming reality. All that remained was the formality of approval by the United States Congress. That was all but assured. President-elect James K. Polk had won mostly on the basis of the Texas issue. It had been a narrow victory, but it was still a mandate. Now, Americans who had once opposed annexation clamored for it. The British and French were trying desperately to block the move, but Jack knew they were too late. Mexico had offered a full independence treaty to Texas; that was rejected out of hand.

The war clouds were building. And when the first thunderclap came, the Rangers would be called.

Jack closed and locked the desk drawer containing his copies of official reports and confidential correspondence. He strode through the door into the soft autumn glow which caressed the crowded San Antonio streets.

He found Sam Walker in front of Antonio Perez's store, swearing in a new recruit. Jack waited until Sam dismissed the man, then strode to Walker's side. "I need a favor, Sam," he said.

"Just name it, Jack."

"We both know Taylor's going to yell for help soon, Sam. When we go into Mexico, we'll need every hole card we can get. I want you to go back East again. Hunt up Samuel Colt and tell him we need a thousand more of these." Jack tapped the butt of the Walker Colt at his belt. "Taylor doesn't care for them for his own troops, but he's authorized us to order the guns for Ranger use. Come back as soon as you can. I don't know when this war will start, but when Taylor yelps, we won't have much time to pull our people together. Bigfoot can take over your company until you return."

Sam Walker cocked an eye at Jack. "You know something the rest of us don't?"

"I know a little. I guess at a lot."

"That's good enough for me, Jack. I'll be on my way in an hour."

Jack watched Walker stride away, then started back to his office. At the corner of the central plaza he paused and stared toward the Council House and the flag of the Republic of Texas waving lazily in the lingering Indian Summer breeze. In a few weeks, he thought, that flag will come down. In its place of honor would be the Stars and Stripes of the United States of America, the sixth national banner to be hoisted above the soil of Texas. *It has to be,* he reminded himself, *but I'm going to miss that flag; there was something special about the Republic of Texas.*

San Antonio
April 1846

Jack Hays rubbed a hand across tired eyes and tried to ignore the headache pounding at his temples. He pushed aside the mound of reports that seemed to breed like rabbits when he wasn't watching.

From all accounts, General Zachary Taylor was headed for trouble. The American force had moved south from Corpus Christi to Port Isabel, barely a rifle shot from the Rio Grande, and established a fort under the command of Major Jacob Brown directly across the river from Matamoros. Mexico's General Mariano Arista, with an army of infantry, dragoons, lancers and cannon, had moved into position near Matamoros. Jack could almost smell the powder smoke.

"Major Hays?"

A young courier in the uniform of an American Army dragoon private stood in the doorway, dispatch case in hand.

"I'm Jack Hays. Come in, please."

The courier pulled a packet from the dispatch case. "Message for you, sir. From General Zachary Taylor."

Jack took the packet and waved toward a seat. "If you don't mind, sir, I'll stand," the private said. "I'm to return to General Taylor with your acknowledgment of receipt of the packet."

Jack checked the seal to verify the authenticity of the packet, then sliced it open with his belt knife and scanned the document. Sixty dragoons under Taylor's command had been captured by Mexican troops while on scout along the Rio Grande, and Arista had opened a bombardment of the post manned by Major Brown.

Two paragraphs seemed to leap off the page:

I have informed Washington by packet that hostilities may now be considered commenced.

So, Jack thought, *the war's now officially underway.*

As commanding general, I have requested the governor of Texas raise four regiments, two of horse and two of foot, for the engagement with Mexico. I ask that you oversee the formation of a mounted regiment with your frontier Texas Ranger force as the nucleus, and that you then report in person to me as a consultant and valued adjutant in the conduct of this campaign. You will be commissioned a Colonel of the United States Army, with all authorities and privileges thereto attaining.

The message bore the signature of General Zachary Taylor.

Jack refolded the message and tucked it into a shirt pocket, then reached for pen and paper. He wrote a brief one-paragraph acknowledgment of his receipt of the orders, dated it, puffed the ink dry and handed it to the private.

Jack sat silent behind the desk for a few minutes after the courier had left. Then he reached again for pen and paper, and wrote:

Dear Susan,

It pains me deeply to say I will not be able to visit you for some time. The war we both knew was coming has arrived. I do not know when I will be able to see you again, or how long I will be away. But I will be with you in spirit and you will be foremost in my mind, my comfort in the trying days to come. Please understand this separation is not of my choosing, but a duty which I cannot deny.

Jack agonized for several long moments over how he should close the letter, torn between what he longed to say and what would be proper. Finally, he dipped the pen in the inkwell. "To hell with propriety," he muttered aloud, "this may be my last chance to say it."

He closed with:

All my love,
JACK

He was surprised that the word *love* flowed so easily from the pen. It hadn't been nearly as difficult to say as he had thought it would be. He addressed the envelope to Miss Susan Calvert,

Seguin, Texas. He caught the mail coach just before it pulled away from the San Antonio station for the twice-weekly run through Seguin and to points east.

He watched in silence until the coach disappeared from view, then strode back to his office. There was no time to waste; putting together a regiment of good and qualified men was not a task done overnight. And in the meantime, he would be stuck in San Antonio, miles from the action. It grated on the nerves.

San Antonio
July 1846

A trickle of sweat edged down Jack Hays's back as he stood before twenty men who had ridden in from the Blanco River area in response to his call for volunteers. He was satisfied with this group; they would fill out his final company. "Gentlemen," Jack said, "you are now members of the First Texas Volunteer Mounted Regiment. In three days we ride to join General Zachary Taylor's army of invasion in the war with Mexico."

A couple of the younger recruits cheered. The veterans showed little outward emotion other than the narrowing of eyes and clenching of jaw muscles.

"You may set up camp anywhere you wish. The Council House is available if you would like to spend a couple of nights indoors. It may be the last time we sleep under a roof for a long time to come."

Jack dismissed the men and returned to his office to finish the paperwork which followed the swearing in of the new Rangers. It had been an almost daily routine for weeks now. Names, hometowns, next of kin—or friends if the recruit had no living relatives—and a list of equipment, description and value of horses, and other personal effects of each man. For a surveyor and engineer, whose life was at least half paper, Jack thought, he had developed a growing aversion to forms and reports.

He cleaned and stowed the pen, rose and began pacing the floor. It was another daily battle to be fought, the struggle against restlessness and impatience. His work here was done, and Jack Hays wanted to be on his way to Mexico.

Rangers had been filtering down to Zachary Taylor's army since the flag of the Republic had been lowered. They went by companies, by pairs and as individual horsemen, and already they had served Taylor well.

Sam Walker had gone directly to Taylor's camp on the Rio Grande upon his return from New Jersey, raising a Ranger company on the way. Walker's men had snaked through miles of the mesquite and chaparral of the no-man's-land between the Nueces and the Rio Grande, kept Taylor advised of Mexican troop movements and scouted out the best routes for the American Army to follow. Walker himself had slipped through hundreds of Mexican soldiers to relay situation reports from Major Brown to General Taylor.

Taylor had fought off Arista's army at Palo Alto Prairie on May 7, inflicting more damage than he sustained. Two days later, Taylor's flying artillery units mauled Arista badly at Resaca de la Palma. Fort Brown had held against the Mexican siege and bombardment, although Major Brown had been killed in the battle. Arista pulled his battered army back to Monterrey, a hundred sixty miles away across some of the most forbidding land known to man.

Now, Taylor was holding his ground as he planned his campaign to carry the war to Arista and take Monterrey.

Ben McCulloch and his company of Rangers from the Guadalupe area had been in Matamoros since late May, probing Mexican troop strength and scouting routes of approach to Monterrey.

Jack Hays could only read the reports and follow the campaign in his mind as he built the Texas Mounted Regiment from his San Antonio headquarters, far from the battles in the sprawling Mustang Desert. He knew his role in San Antonio was crucial to the success of the campaign. His efforts had given Sam and Ben reinforcements of seasoned and competent frontiersmen skilled in the art of war against Mexicans. Most of his own regiment now awaited Jack's arrival in Mexico. Still, the job in San Antonio grated on Jack's nerves. He knew himself well enough to know why. He felt he was sending his men into danger while he stayed snug in his own quarters. It was a sense of betrayal that lay heavy in Jack's gut.

A clatter of hooves and screech of wooden brakes against wheel rims in the street outside the office cut through Jack's melancholy. He stepped to the doorway. The mail coach rocked gently on its traces as the driver stepped down from his perch, flashed a gap-toothed grin at Jack and waved toward the rear of the coach. "Present for you, Major Hays," the driver said. "From Miss Susan Calvert."

Behind the coach, the rangy black horse called Justin tossed its head and snorted.

Jack stood silent for a moment, surprised.

"Well, Major, don't just stand there. Unhitch the beast." The driver dug into a mail pouch and came out with a handful of letters and official-looking documents and handed the bundle to Jack. "Sure wish I had a pretty woman giving me horses," he said with a chuckle. "Had the devil's own time trying to figure what the postage was on a black horse. Finally said the hell with it and let him tag along for free. Go ahead, Major Hays. Fetch your horse. I'm running late and people are waiting on their mail."

Jack untied the lead rope and ran a hand along the black's neck. The horse snuffled and nosed Jack's shoulder. Jack couldn't tell if the horse was greeting him or just scratching an itch. The coach clattered away.

Jack sorted quickly through the stack of mail, found Susan's letter, opened it and read the delicate, flowing script as he led the black toward the stable behind the office. He read the closing paragraphs several times:

Please accept this gift of Justin as a token of my love, Jack. I know you are fond of him, and I pray he will carry you safely home to me after the war is ended.

I only hope that each time you ride him, you will think of me. My thoughts and my love will be with you in the desperate times ahead.

The message was signed simply, "With Love, SUSAN."

Jack swallowed against the lump in his throat. He tucked the letter into his breast pocket and patted the black's shoulder. "Well, Justin Otherhorse," he said, his voice soft, "it looks like you and I have a long ride ahead. I hope you like Mexico."

THIRTEEN

Camargo, Mexico
July 1846

Jack Hays clamped a hand on the body behind the Camargo stables and flipped it over. The bullet had hit the Mexican an inch above the left eye and tore away a fist-sized chunk of skull as it exited above the right ear. Blood and brain matter still oozed from the wound. The damage looked like what one would expect from a big-bore pistol fired at close range. Like a Walker Colt.

Jack stepped away from the body and glanced around the half circle of bearded faces standing by the dead man. "Anyone here know this man?"

Alligator Davis nodded. "He was at Reynosa. Called himself *El Carnicero*. The Butcher. One of the civilian guards of the Mier bunch. Took a bullwhip to Bigfoot Wallace. Damn near beat Bigfoot to death." Davis spat a stream of tobacco juice onto the dead man's chest. "Wasn't too kind to the rest of us, either."

"Colonel Hays!" A breathless young Army dragoon lieutenant pushed his way into the crowd of Rangers. "General Taylor would like to see you, Colonel. Now."

General Zachary Taylor stood behind the folding table which served as his desk and glared at Jack Hays.

The general's close-set eyes, high cheekbones, long nose and broad chin might have been carved from Maine granite instead of the gentle, rolling hills of his native Virginia. Jack wondered idly if there might be some Indian blood in Taylor's veins; he looked more like a Cherokee chief than an American general.

The general was not pleased.

"Colonel Hays, this slaughter of innocent Mexican civilians must stop. Immediately. This is the sixth man found dead in this village alone, and God knows how many your Rangers killed in Reynosa. It's simply inhuman. It's an embarrassment to the Army of Occupation and a violation of the rules of war."

Jack kept his face impassive. "I arrived here only a few days ago, General, so I don't know about the ones at Reynosa," he said, "but this latest dead man was a party to the mistreatment of the Mier Expedition captives. So were three of the others. A fifth was a known gunrunner feeding rifles to the Comanches for Canales. I suspect the dead men at Reynosa had adequate reason for earning a pistol ball. I wouldn't exactly call them innocent."

Taylor leaned forward, fists clenched, knuckles white against the tabletop. "Colonel Hays, I asked for your Rangers of necessity, not by preference. Unfortunately, my initial reservations have been verified by their conduct."

Jack felt the anger flare in his gut. He hadn't raised a regiment and ridden for days just to get his butt chewed by some general who wouldn't be able to find the next water hole without the Rangers. A man didn't criticize a Texas Ranger until he had earned the right.

"General, many of these Rangers are survivors of Mier and Perote. Many others lost friends and relatives at the Alamo, at Goliad or at Salado Creek. They recognize only one rule of war. That, sir, is victory. Retribution goes hand in glove with victory where this particular war is concerned, at least as my men see it." Jack kept his voice calm with a conscious effort.

"Nonetheless, Colonel, I expect you to maintain discipline among your Rangers. I want you to issue a direct order that no other Mexicans are to be molested. Is that understood?"

"I'll issue the order, General."

Zachary Taylor snorted in disgust. "And, no doubt, it will be ignored. Colonel Hays, I find your men woefully short of discipline, resentful of authority and direct orders and, to a great extent, contemptuous of their counterparts in the U.S. Army."

Jack glared back at the general. "And how do you rate them as a fighting force, sir?"

The slightest hint of a smile flickered in Zachary Taylor's eyes. "Superb, Colonel. Absolutely superb." Taylor leaned away from the desk and seemed to relax. The deep frown lines eased. "Colonel Hays, I freely admit that I've observed no more competent scouts or braver men than Sam Walker, Ben McCulloch and Richard Gillespie. If the Texas Rangers would only accept discipline and military subordination, they would be the finest light cavalry fighting force on the face of this man's earth."

Jack took a deep breath and let the coals of his anger cool. "I don't wish to contradict you, General. But they already *are* the finest light cavalry on earth."

Zachary Taylor shook his head in resignation. "Very well, Colonel. I'll concede that point. Still, I would send every Texas Ranger in this camp packing except for one thing."

"What might that be, General?"

"I want to win this damn war."

Two hours later, Jack Hays squatted on his heels, surrounded by Rangers. "Men," he said solemnly, "I have been instructed to issue you strict orders not to molest any unarmed Mexican civilians." He raised a hand to quiet the murmur of protest. "Now, let me finish. You are not to molest them. But if the body of a man known to have been involved with the torture or execution of Texans should be found in the brush"—Jack paused for a moment to shake his head in mock sadness—"I believe we may safely conclude that, in a fit of remorse over his misdeeds and tormented by his conscience, he has taken his own life. *¿Quién sabe?*"

Camargo, Mexico
August 1846

Ben McCulloch rode into Camargo with the brim of his hat turned up. Jack Hays knew how to read that sign. Ben was in a sour mood. Jack fell into step as Ben strode toward the general's command headquarters. "Trouble, Ben?"

Ben snorted in disgust. "I almost had him, Jack. That damn Juan Seguin. I missed him by maybe three days at China."

Jack shook his head in silent sympathy. The Rangers wanted Seguin badly. The former Texas patriot had gone over to the other side four years ago and now operated a band of irregulars, mostly bandits, from his headquarters in the China area.

"Worse than that was missing Canales," Ben grumbled. "I thought I had the bastard cornered back in June and I came up empty then, too. Seems like I'm always caught with a pair of deuces when everybody else has aces in this game."

Ben's weariness showed beneath the deep frown in his sun-bronzed face; his shoulders slumped and he shuffled a bit when he walked. "Two hundred fifty miles in ten days, and I haven't had my boots off the whole time. At least we found out how we can, and how we can't, get to Monterrey."

Jack listened in silence as Ben made his brief report to Zachary Taylor. The route through China would not support an entire army; a regiment, maybe. The Linares route wouldn't support a coyote, let alone an army. The only route with ample water and forage was from Camargo to Mier, then south through Cerralvo to Marin, less than thirty miles from Monterrey.

"Thank you, Captain McCulloch," Taylor said. "Your services are deeply appreciated. You and your men get what rest you can. This evening we will plan our approach to Monterrey."

China, Mexico
August 1846

Jack Hays shifted his weight in the saddle and watched as the Army dragoon regiment filed past into the village of China. Jack, his regiment of Rangers and four hundred dragoons from the regular Army ranks had been assigned the southern route to Monterrey. Their job was to intercept any Mexican force headed toward the main body of American troops to the north. Jack had also taken the opportunity to scout the countryside for Seguin and Canales. He'd had no more luck than Ben. It was as if the chaparral had swallowed both the fugitives.

To the north, Taylor's army moved along the San Juan Valley, with Ben McCulloch and Richard Gillespie leading the advance as scouts. Sam Walker's company pulled double duty as scouts and couriers between the two forces. If all went according to plan, the two American columns would converge in two or three weeks at San Francisco, within sight of the mountains guarding Monterrey.

The slow pace of the advance grated on Jack's nerves. He was more at home with the fast ride and quick, bloody strike of the Rangers. But he had to match his pace to that of Taylor's troops, and moving an army of six thousand men, most of them afoot, into place for the siege of a heavily fortified and defended city was a different animal than taking sixty men into a raid on a hundred Mexican soldiers. He had to play the Army's game this time.

Quartermaster Henry Whiting rode to Jack's side. Whiting rode surprisingly well for a regular Army man. "Problem up ahead, Colonel," Whiting said, mopping the sweat from his forehead with a neckerchief. "We need about forty more mules. There's plenty of them in China, but the mayor there says there are none for sale."

Jack tugged at the brim of his hat and smiled. "No problem, Quartermaster. Take me to the *alcalde*. I will reason with him."

The *alcalde* of China stood behind the bar of the cantina, idly wiping a glass with a frayed towel. He glanced up as Jack stepped from the bright sunlight of the street into the semi-darkness of the adobe building.

"Señor Calasos?"

"*Sí.* Come in, come in. Something to drink? A cold *cerveza*, perhaps?"

Jack strode to the bar. The place was all but empty in the heat of the day, the time of *siesta*. Two Mexicans dressed in the costume of *vaqueros* lounged at a corner table. "Nothing to drink, thank you." Jack saw the smile fade from Calasos's face. "I come to pay my respects to the *alcalde* of China, and to discuss business with him." Jack half-turned at the bar, his right hand resting near the butt of the Walker Colt at his belt. He made sure the two *vaqueros* saw the movement. "I have come to buy some mules. My name is Jack Hays."

The two *vaqueros* sat bolt upright at the mention of the name. Much of the color drained from Calasos's face.

"Señor Hays," Calasos said, his voice quavering, "your name is not unknown here. But alas, there are no mules for sale in China."

At the corner of his vision Jack saw one of the *vaqueros* reach toward his belt. He spun to face the man. "Touch the pistol and your wife is a widow, friend," he said in Spanish. The man slowly raised his hands and placed them palm down on the table. Jack gestured with his head toward the door. "Come with me, *alcalde*. There is something I would show you." He nodded toward the two *vaqueros*. "Perhaps you gentlemen will join us?"

Jack herded the two *vaqueros* before him, Calasos at his side. He heard a sharp intake of breath from one of the *vaqueros*. *"Rinche,"* the man said. *"Los diablos Tejanos."*

"Yes, my friend. Rangers. The Texas devils."

In the center of the street two dozen Texas Rangers sat on their saddles and stared at the trio of Mexicans. *Damn if they wouldn't scare me a little bit, too,* Jack thought; *meanest-looking, dirtiest bunch of ruffians as I've ever seen.* Jack dismissed the two *vaqueros* as a threat. They knew that any move beyond a belch would bring them so much lead that nine men would be needed to carry their caskets.

"Mayor Calasos," he said in Spanish, "you have a pleasant little town here." He kept his voice low. "It would be a shame to see it reduced to rubble. If these men here—" he gestured toward the Rangers "—were to suspect your town had harbored soldiers from, say, Goliad. Or possibly Perote Prison . . ." Jack let his voice trail away, studying the *alcalde*'s face. Calasos had turned almost white; his prominent Adam's apple bobbed nervously.

Jack let him sweat for a few more heartbeats. "Now we will talk of mules. The United States Army is prepared to pay twenty-five dollars in silver for each good work mule. It is a fair price."

"But there are no—"

"Perhaps someone here," Jack interrupted, "even served with General Woll in the invasion of San Antonio." Jack sighed. "That would greatly upset my men. The price is now twenty-three dollars per mule."

"Señor Hays, I—do not—" The *alcalde* stammered in confusion and growing desperation.

"Twenty-two dollars each," Jack said. "Forty head. Delivered at sundown to the China plaza. Until then I can control my men. But after then, who knows?" He punctuated the question with a laconic Mexican-style shrug.

"Señor Hays, please—for you I will find the mules."

Jack draped his arm around the *alcalde*'s shoulders. "Ah, Señor Calasos, I knew I could count on you, once you came to see how badly my men need these mules. Until sundown, then?"

The sun was still an hour above the mountains to the west as Jack watched Quartermaster Whiting count out the silver for the payment of the last mule.

"Dammit, Jack," Alligator Davis grouched, "I halfway wish they hadn't decided to come across. Tearing up this town would have been fun."

"Yes, 'Gator, it would have," Jack said almost wistfully. "But for now we need the mules more than the entertainment. Fun's fun, but Monterrey calls."

Monterrey, Mexico
September 1846

Jack Hays tightened the cinch on Justin, heard the black's grunt of disapproval and swung into the saddle. He raised a hand and waved the column forward.

The night had been miserable. Not a man in Jack's command had managed to stay dry and warm in the driving rainstorm that built over the Sierra Madre at dusk and raked the American troops throughout the night. Jack had a feeling the day might turn out even worse.

Monterrey is going to be one tough nut to crack, he thought. The city of fifteen thousand civilians, swollen by half again that number of Mexican troops, nested on the north bank of the swift waters of the Santa Clara River in the Sierra Madre foothills. A level plain, crossed by the roads from Marin and Monclova, sprawled to the north. On the west, Independence Hill provided a strong defensive position, while the peaks of the Sierra Madre protected the south and east. American Army engineers and Sam Walker's scouts had mapped out the Mexican defenses. General Pedro de Ampudia had turned the city into a fortress.

From numerous councils of war in Taylor's camp had come the decision. A frontal assault along the Cerralvo Road, against Ampudia's heaviest fortifications, would leave the American Army with such heavy losses it might never recover. Instead, Taylor's army was split into two units; Taylor would keep the Mexicans busy at the main entrance to the city, while General William J. Worth's unit, led by four hundred Texas Rangers from Jack's command, bypassed Monterrey to the north, then turned south to cut the Saltillo Road and attack the city from the least expected quarter—the west.

The only problems with the plan, Jack thought, were Independence Hill, crowned by the heavily fortified Bishop's Palace on the north bank of the Santa Clara, and the solid defenses on Federation Hill on the south bank. But Monterrey *had* to be taken. The army that controlled Monterrey controlled northern Mexico. It was that simple. The success of the whole campaign rested with Jack's Rangers and General Worth's two thousand regular and volunteer infantrymen.

At Jack's left rode Ben McCulloch, at his right Richard Gillespie, with Thad Green close behind. Bigfoot Wallace had the point, riding alone to scout ahead of the main column. Jack wished he had Sam Walker along as well, but Sam's talents were needed elsewhere.

Heavy clouds blanketed the sky and a thick mist kept the chill on the still-soaked American column. The sounds of an army on the march seemed muted by the heavy, wet air. The Saltillo Road was only a few hundred yards ahead.

Richard Gillespie suddenly checked his mount, turned his head and listened intently. Jack could make out the faint thud of hooves in the distance. "Company coming, Captain Jack," Gillespie said. "If it isn't Bigfoot, we're in trouble. If it is, fast as that horse is moving, we're still in trouble."

The hoofbeats grew louder. A moment later Bigfoot Wallace pulled his big dun to a mud-slinging stop. "Mess of Mexicans up ahead, Jack. I make it a couple hundred lancers, about two, three times that many foot soldiers behind 'em.''

Jack nodded. "Pass the word for a final weapons check," he said to Ben and Gillespie. "Let the men know what we're riding into. We'll hit them as soon as we see them."

Ten minutes later Jack spotted the scarlet coats of the Mexican lancers, a blur in the mist. A gust of breeze pushed a small opening in the fog and drizzle. Jack glimpsed the gaudy uniform of a Mexican colonel astride a compact Spanish horse. The lancers were moving into formation, awaiting the sound of the bugle to charge. The infantry would be close behind the lancers, Jack knew. He could be leading his men into a trap; there might be a division of dragoons and infantry waiting just up the trail. There wasn't time to worry about it now.

Jack pulled the Walker Colt from its holster and drew the hammer to full cock. "Charge them!" he yelled.

The Texan war cry hammered against the low clouds and seemed to echo back down onto the open plain over the pound of hooves on the soggy turf. The lancers wasted a few crucial seconds as the last horsemen fell into skirmish formation before the sound of the bugle cut through the heavy air. The lancer colonel raised his saber.

The range closed to forty yards. Jack reined Justin sharply to his left and snapped a shot at the lancer captain. He knew the shot had gone wild even as the Walker bucked against his palm. Along the Texas line, handguns barked. Two lancers tumbled from their horses and a third went down with his mount. Jack thumbed the hammer and fired again, saw a lancer's horse stumble under the impact of the heavy ball. Then Jack's horse crashed into the front line of lancers. A spear point slipped past Jack's ear as he fired into a Mexican's body less than an arm's length away. The shock of the powerful slug slammed the lancer from the saddle. A saber blade flashed at Jack's left. He jammed his right knee into Justin's side; the black lunged toward the swordsman and slammed into the lighter Mexican mount, spilling horse and rider. Jack shot the downed man.

The Texans' charge crumpled the Mexican formation. The battle was man-to-man, Ranger and lancer looking into the face of the man each wanted to kill. Jack emptied his Colt, jammed it into his holster and pulled his second pistol. Quick glimpses of the fight swirling about him registered in Jack's brain—Richard Gillespie dismounting, drawing a careful bead and sending a pistol ball through the head of the lancer colonel; Bigfoot Wallace slapping aside a lance and ripping a Mexican almost in half with the big Bowie knife; 'Gator Davis's whoop of exuberance as he spurred his bay into a knot of lancers; Thad Green, bridle reins held in his teeth, firing calmly and methodically with both hands, choosing his targets; Ben McCulloch surrounded by Mexicans and cut off from the main body of Rangers, then fighting his way clear, leaving three men dead in his wake.

The Mexicans on the fringe of the battle broke and ran, lances and swords tossed aside as they leaned over the necks of their horses in flight. Jack shouted the signal to break off the attack. By the time Jack had reorganized his men and started to count casualties, General Worth's infantry units were pouring onto the battlefield, moving at double time toward the Mexican foot soldiers. The Mexican infantry put up a spirited fight for a few minutes, then panicked as the horde of blue-clad American troops stormed toward them. The Mexican retreat quickly turned into a full-fledged race to the rear.

Thad Green had kept alive his tradition of leaving a piece of himself on every battlefield. Jack tugged a bandage into place over a saber gash on the young man's shoulder. The wound wasn't serious. "Dammit, Thad," Jack grumbled, "you better find a new hobby. There's chunks of you scattered from here to the headwaters of the San Saba."

Jack glanced up as General Worth reined his big gray horse to a stop. "A magnificent fight your men put up, Colonel Hays," Worth said. "Your casualties?"

"Two dead, four wounded," Jack said. "We had ten horses killed or crippled."

Jack and the general surveyed the battlefield and the road beyond. Thirty-five lancers lay dead on the field. A dozen more were covered by Ranger guns, hands atop their heads in surrender. Worth's infantry had mauled the retreating Mexican soldiers in the running fight along the trail. Altogether, more than a hundred Mexicans had died.

An hour later, the mist had stopped, the clouds overhead

thinned and the Saltillo Road was in American hands. Ampudia's supply and communication line was cut.

It wasn't, Jack thought, all that much of a bargain.

He winced as a Mexican cannonball whistled overhead.

"Dammit, there wasn't supposed to be artillery on Federation Hill," Worth snapped. "Now they've got us in a cross fire from Independence and Federation." He yelled to his officers to keep the men under cover, then turned to Jack. "Colonel Hays, we can't just sit here and get cut to pieces by cannon. Can your Texans lead an assault on Federation? I'll give you all the support I can muster."

Jack studied the rocky, brooding cliffs of Federation Hill. It would be a foot operation. The men would have to cross the waist-deep river under fire from the hill, work their way to the crest while exposed to sharpshooters in the breastworks, then finally storm the top.

"General," he said, "my men prefer to fight on horseback. But show them a Mexican and they'll fight any damn way they have to. We can take it."

Jack Hays pressed his body against a boulder halfway up the face of Federation Hill, soaked to the bone and gasping to pull air into tortured lungs. A rifle ball spanged against the rocks near his shoulder.

Bigfoot Wallace lay on his back at Jack's side, rifle resting across his massive, heaving chest. "Dammit, Jack," Bigfoot gasped, "if the—good Lord had meant—me to be climbin' rock —he'd of made me a billy goat—'stead of a Texas Ranger." A rifle slug kicked dirt over Bigfoot's outsized moccasin. "Now, that's gettin' too damn personal," Bigfoot grumbled. "That's one Mexican can shoot." He flopped over onto his stomach and cocked the long rifle. "Suck him out for me, Jack."

Jack struggled to his feet, stepped to the side of the boulder and snapped a pistol shot toward the ridge. A head poked over the redoubt. Bigfoot's rifle boomed. The Mexican rifleman's head exploded like a ripe melon. "That's one good Mexican," Bigfoot said as he reached for his ammunition pouch.

Both men's breathing had returned to normal by the time

Bigfoot reloaded and capped the rifle. "Cap'n Jack, how's about you and me go make some more good Mexicans?"

Jack glanced toward a group of men thirty yards to his left. "Looks like Ben's bunch is ready to go." Jack waved a hand in a circle and saw Ben's answering wave. "Well, Bigfoot, as the man said, it's all uphill from here. Sic 'em."

Jack's company and Ben's unit topped the Federation Hill redoubt a few seconds ahead of a Louisiana volunteer infantry unit. A dismounted regular Army artillery company followed close behind. The flat blast of Louisiana horse pistols mingled with the throaty roar of Walker Colts and the deeper thump of shotguns. A few of the defenders died where they lay; others fled their posts, bolting for the safety of Fort Soldado six hundred yards away on the other end of the hill. The battle at the crest of Federation Hill was as bloody as it was quick, the Texans' war whoops in sharp contrast to the near silence of the deadly efficient Louisianans. The Ranger charge swept over the Mexican cannoneers. One of the American artillery officers shouted orders; gun crews put their shoulders into the weapons. The heavy guns swung toward the fort at the far end of the hill. Moments later the captured cannon launched their first balls toward the Mexican soldiers fleeing toward Fort Soldado. Rangers and uniformed American troops did not pause in their assault, pouring across the open ground in pursuit.

Richard Gillespie was the first man to top the breastworks of Fort Soldado; his company was the first to fight its way inside the fort proper.

Jack Hays leaned against a wall, letting his breathing return to normal as he reloaded his Colts. An occasional gunshot or shouted command was all that remained of the assault on the fort. Before sundown, General Worth's regimental colors would fly over Fort Soldado. Gillespie had earned the honor of hoisting the colors.

Bigfoot Wallace picked up a dead Mexican soldier, dropped the body atop two others and sat on the bloody mound. The frontiersman wiped the blade of his Bowie knife on a dead man's shirt, carved a chunk from his plug and popped the tobacco chew into his mouth.

"Comfortable, Bigfoot?"

Bigfoot squinted up at Jack. "Yep. Downright cozy. Like a circuit preacher with a plate of fried chicken."

Jack rammed the final load home, capped the cylinders and dropped the revolver into its holster.

"Don't get too relaxed, friend," Jack said. "I just got word by messenger. We've got to go back down the hill. We did such a good job here that General Worth wants us to do it again. At Independence."

Bigfoot spat a stream of tobacco juice onto the back of a dead man's head. "Jack," he said wistfully, "sometimes I wish we weren't so damned good."

FOURTEEN

Monterrey, Mexico
September 1846

Jack Hays clawed his way through the loose shale, rifle balls kicking near his shoulder and hip, and threw himself to the ground behind a juniper bush in a rocky outcrop, legs trembling and lungs shrieking for air.

Federation Hill was a picnic compared to this chunk of rock, he thought. The northwest slope of Independence Hill was almost straight up, rocky and rugged. His men were as exhausted as he was, and they still had forty yards to go. The Mexican sharpshooters atop the hill were good. Jack had a sixty-four-caliber hole in the brim of his hat to attest to that fact. He chanced a quick look over the juniper. Sam Walker's Ranger company, brought in to help the assault, inched its way up the steep face to his left; at his right Richard Gillespie's men scratched and clawed toward the heights. Close behind the Rangers were two hundred fifty Army regulars and the Louisiana men. As usual, Bigfoot Wallace was at Jack's side. The big scout flashed a tobacco-stained grin. Wallace's massive chest heaved.

"Makes a man—appreciate—a good horse," Bigfoot gasped, "and them—infantry boys—too. But, by God no—foot soldier gonna—beat us to the top." He thumbed back the hammer of his rifle. "Ready when—you are, boss."

Jack pulled his Colt. "Let's go get 'em."

The attackers crabbed up the hillside, slugs tearing down at them from the heights above. Twenty yards from the top, Jack heard Richard Gillespie's wild whoop; the whole attack force seemed to catch its second wind in a sprint toward the parapet above. The Americans had not fired a shot during the long climb. Now muzzles flashed and smoke billowed along the entire line. The Mexican troops held in the face of superior firepower for a tense, bloody moment before the Rangers swept over the top. Crumpled bodies littered the upper parapet. The surviving defenders fell back toward the Bishop's Castle at the far end of the hill; a rear guard put up a half-hearted stand before panic overtook them. The retreat became a sprint for survival for the Mexican troops.

Jack stood amid the carnage, smoke curling from the muzzle of his Walker. His legs wobbled in exhaustion. He knew the Americans were simply too tired to pursue. The Bishop's Castle would have to wait.

A final rattle of gunfire echoed from atop the ridge of Independence Hill. Jack sat down to massage life back into his aching legs. A deathly silence gripped the hill for several seconds, then a cheer from hundreds of parched throats shattered the quiet. Jack glanced toward Gillespie's position. The Stars and Stripes fluttered from a staff in Gillespie's hand on Independence Hill.

An answering cheer came back from the American troops now occupying Federation. Jack checked the impulse to add his own yell of exuberance to the din. Independence Hill had been breached, but it hadn't been taken. The Bishop's Palace still waited, brooding and malevolent, more than a quarter mile away beyond the stunted trees, heavy brush and boulders flanking a narrow road to the fortress.

The order to stand down and rest rippled through the American lines. Jack's breathing had returned to normal by the time the colonel in command of the Army assault forces made his way to Jack's post.

"Colonel Hays, I'm afraid we've more trouble on the way. One of your scouts has spotted reinforcements, infantry and horse, moving up from Monterrey toward the fort. It looks like we're in for a counterattack." The officer paused to mop sweat and grime from his forehead. "I've sent runners for Captain Gillespie and Lieutenant Colonel Walker. We've got a little war parley ahead."

Jack crouched behind a jumble of rocks and brush at the side of the narrow road. The sun was approaching its midpoint, adding thirst to the exhaustion of the hard climb and desperate fight on Independence Hill.

The plan should work, Jack thought. It was a simple ambush. Jack's Rangers were concealed in the brush along one side of the road, Sam's men on the other, regular Army troops interspersed with the Rangers. To anyone observing from the Bishop's Palace, it would seem the Texans had withdrawn down the hill, leaving behind only a couple of hundred Louisiana volunteers.

Jack heard the bugle sound at the Palace. The word soon came in whispers down the line. The Mexicans were coming.

Jack waited, listening to the thud of his own heart, as the first hoofbeats sounded along the road. He waited as the Louisiana troops cautiously retreated, waited as a Mexican heavy cavalry company followed by light horse troops filed past, sunlight dancing from broadswords and lances, waited as the infantry marched into view, weapons and brilliant uniforms glittering in the sun. The Louisianans fell back almost to the lip of Independence Hill, stalked by the confident Mexican troops, when Sam Walker's battle yell sounded.

Within a heartbeat, a deadly fire from the concealed Americans raked the Mexican flanks and the Louisiana troops opened up on the enemy from the front. Dozens of Mexican soldiers fell in the first few seconds of the ambush; some infantrymen were run down by their own cavalry as the horsemen whirled and spurred horses back toward the fort.

The blistering fire of the American force decimated the Mexican formation. Survivors threw down their guns and sprinted toward the fort. Some of them reached it just as the first shell from Worth's light howitzer company tore into the earthwork in front of the castle. Shells from the captured cannon on Federation Hill joined in, pounding the Mexican stronghold.

"Charge!"

With the shout from the American lines, Rangers and Army troops poured from the ambush site toward the fort. Stragglers from the ambushed Mexican units fell before the pistols and swords of the attackers. Musket fire rattled from the defenders of the fort's outer breastworks, answered by American rifles, as grape and ball from Mexican cannons burst among the attackers. A howitzer round from Worth's artillery below shattered the heavy doors of the castle. The American charge swept over the outer defenses and into Bishop's Castle itself. Sharp, bloody hand-to-hand battles unfolded in the choking powder smoke inside the walls.

Bishop's Castle was in American hands at mid-afternoon. The victory was not without its price. Eighteen Americans had died in the assault, among them Texas Ranger Captain Richard Addison Gillespie. Once again, he had been the first man to breach the walls. His body lay among those of five Mexican soldiers. Jack counted seventeen bullet or bayonet wounds in the big Ranger's body. Richard Gillespie had taken a lot of killing.

The sun had not set before reinforcements poured into the Palace and the Independence Hill redoubts. Weary Texans, many with tears flowing unashamed from dirty, powder-burned, blood-smeared faces, stood guard over Gillespie's body and four other fallen Rangers. Jack leaned exhausted against a bullet-scarred wall, the smell of battle still heavy in his nostrils. His ears whined from the concussion of big-bore weapons fired at close range in a confined space. He wanted nothing more than to care for his men, to sleep—

"Colonel Hays?"

Jack nodded, took a slip of paper from General Worth's messenger and scanned the contents. "Tell the General his orders are received and understood." Jack did not look up as he spoke.

"Yes, sir."

Jack waited until the messenger's footfalls faded beyond the buzz in his ears, then pushed himself away from the wall. He found Sam Walker and Bigfoot Wallace.

"Sorry to tell you this, men," Jack said, "but we've got to go down the mountain again."

"Aw, what the hell now, Jack?" Bigfoot groused. "Worth find us another hill to climb?"

"More or less. It seems we're going to be the first to ride into Monterrey."

Bigfoot Wallace sighed in relief. "At least the damn streets are flat," he said.

Jack Hays jammed the crowbar into the gap between masonry blocks and glanced at Alligator Davis. The husky Ranger pulled back both hammers of the sawed-off double-barrel shotgun and nodded. Mexican muskets boomed in a steady cadence from inside the house.

Jack leaned into the prybar. A yard-square chunk of weakened masonry popped free. Davis jammed the muzzle of the smoothbore into the hole and touched off both barrels. Screams of pain and shock sounded from within the walls. Jack dropped the crowbar, pulled his Walker and sprayed a cylinder load into the room.

The Mexican defenders bolted through the door, only to crumple under a storm of lead from Ranger guns outside. Davis kicked at the hole in the wall. His heavy boots enlarged the opening. Jack switched guns and dove through the hole, rolling on his shoulder on the dirt floor inside.

Four uniformed bodies lay inside the one-room house, riddled by buckshot and pistol balls; one wounded Mexican infantryman struggled to a knee and tried to turn his rifle toward Jack. The Walker slammed into Jack's palm. The slug knocked the soldier against the far wall. Then there was no one left to shoot. One more building had fallen in the desperate battle for Monterrey. Jack reloaded his pistols as Davis rammed fresh charges home in the shotgun.

"Hell of a way to fight a war," Davis said. His cheek bled from a saber nick below the eye. Dirt and powder residue dusted his beard. "Give me a good, clean cavalry charge out in the open anytime." Davis suddenly winked and grinned. "Worst damn thing about it," he said, "is they took their wives and whores out first."

In a temporary lull in the firing outside, Jack heard the distant reports of gunshots from Sam Walker's combined Ranger and Army force a block away to the north.

The Mexicans had dug in around Cemetery Plaza. Adobe and masonry houses were fortified and sandbagged, loopholes for rifles chipped through walls. The battle for Monterrey was now a matter of digging the Mexicans out, taking one house at a time, one street at a time.

American sharpshooters climbed to the rooftops of captured buildings and traded shots with their Mexican counterparts atop the next structure, while other men blasted their way into the houses with makeshift black powder bombs, or chiseled in with crowbars and picks. The Mexican defenders were seasoned infantry, and even the Texans gave them credit for courage under fire. This would be no rout, Jack knew. It was a gut-wrenching battle where you looked into the eyes of the man you were about to kill. You saw fear or anger or resignation in the eyes as you pulled the trigger.

The advance had been faster, if not easier, until General Taylor called off his assault on the other end of town. When the thud of American guns ceased, Ampudia threw his reserves into the fight for Cemetery Plaza.

Jack crouched in the center of the room, feeling the pain of exhaustion in abused shoulder and back muscles. The lowering sun slashed gray-gold rays through the rifle slits along the wall. Swirls and eddies of powder smoke and dust drifted through the narrow bands of sunlight. The coppery smell of blood and the stench of urine and offal released in death throes lay acrid and heavy in Jack's nostrils. *'Gator's right,* he thought, *it's a hell of a way to fight a war.* He shoved himself away from the wall.

"Let's go open up another one, 'Gator," he said.

Jack Hays had never seen Sam Walker so furious. Walker's blue eyes practically flashed fire above his dirty, rust-colored beard. A muscle twitched along Sam's jaw and veins bulged on his neck and forehead.

Jack had to admit he wasn't too pleased himself.

"What the hell do you mean, pull out?" Walker almost shouted the question.

Jack put a hand on Sam's forearm. "Easy, Sam. Don't do anything foolish."

General Worth raised a hand in supplication. "No need to kill the messenger, Colonel Walker. Believe me, it wasn't my idea. We were on the verge of taking all of central Monterrey. Another four days and we'd have pushed Ampudia into General Taylor's guns and wiped out his whole army. But like it or not, General Taylor *is* the commanding officer. The cease-fire was his decision."

Sam Walker's face darkened another shade. "Dammit, General—" Walker took a half step forward. Jack tightened his grip on Sam's arm.

"Sam, we've ridden together a long time," Jack said, "and I'm going to give you my first direct order. Wait outside. Cool off a bit before you do something rash." Walker yanked his arm free of Jack's grip, glared for a moment at the general, then spun and strode from Worth's command headquarters.

"I'll ask you to overlook Sam's outburst, General Worth," Jack said. "I'm sure you understand how he feels. We came into Mexico under the impression we were supposed to *win* the war."

Worth smiled a reassurance. "I understand, Colonel Hays. And I sympathize with Colonel Walker, with you and all the Rangers. We wouldn't have had a snowball's chance without your men. But Ampudia's petitioned General Taylor to let him withdraw the Mexican Army from Monterrey, with honors of war and an eight weeks' truce. Taylor agreed. Technically, Monterrey is now in American hands." Worth's shoulders slumped. "For what it's worth, Jack, I agree with Sam Walker. We've settled for less than a total victory. It's an opportunity lost forever."

Jack tried to shrug away the last of his own anger. "General Worth, I have a regiment of Texas Rangers out there who are mad to the bone. Their feeling—and mine—is that if we aren't allowed to win this war, and since our enlistments are up anyway, we'll just head home to Texas. Somehow, I don't think Zachary Taylor will be overly sad to see us go."

Worth shook Jack's hand. "Maybe General Taylor won't be, Colonel Hays. But there is one general in this man's army who will. There aren't appropriate words to thank you and your men. I'll simply say Godspeed, and may you find all is well at home."

Jack Hays twisted in the saddle for one last look at the City of Monterrey. The Stars and Stripes fluttered from standards across the town. *A lot of good men died here,* Jack thought. His hand fell to the saddlebag where the American flag raised above Federation

Hill by Captain Richard Addison Gillespie rested for the long ride home.

Ben McCulloch reined his horse to a stop alongside Jack and sat quietly for a moment, staring toward Monterrey. "It isn't over, Jack," Ben finally said. "We both know that. And when the fighting starts again, I'll be back."

Ben kicked his horse into motion. Jack watched him ride toward the front of the column of dirty, ragged and grim-faced Rangers.

"I don't doubt that for a minute, Ben," Jack said to himself, "and you won't be alone." Jack nudged the big black into a slow trot. For the first time in weeks, he allowed himself to think seriously of home. And of a slender young woman with the mischievous look of a young colt in her dark eyes and the red-gold touch of sunlight on brown hair.

"Well, Justin," he said to the black, "we've been gone a long time. The Comanches and Mexicans haven't been able to do it; let's just hope some young buck hasn't shot us down in Seguin."

Seguin
March 1847

Jack Hays slouched on the low bench in front of the Calvert home, hoping the tension that had been building in his body didn't show through his attempts to hide it.

He had been calm while digging a Mexican platoon from a storage house in Monterrey. He had been relaxed and confident during the charge that ran down Stone Horse and his band of Paneteka raiders in their camp on Cibolo Creek a week ago.

This was different. All he had to lose during those other encounters was his life.

Susan Calvert's head rested on his shoulder, the scent of her delicate in Jack's nostrils, the touch of her hand warm against his forearm. *Dammit, Jack,* he scolded himself, *you've stalled long enough.* He took a deep breath and tried to will the clammy feeling from his palms.

"Susan, may I ask you something?"

"Ask away, Colonel John Coffee Hays."

"Will you marry me?"

A long silence fell over the Calvert porch. Jack felt the beginnings of despair stir in his gut. *God, she's trying to find a way to say no.* Susan finally lifted her head from his shoulder, raised her face to his. Tears moistened her cheeks. Jack tried to steel himself for the rejection.

"Yes," she said, her voice soft.

"Yes? You will?" Jack knew he hadn't kept the elation from his tone. The emotion was just too powerful. "But why the hesitation, Susan? Have you any doubts?"

"There are times," she said, wiping at a tear with the palm of her free hand, "when a girl needs to try to compose herself before answering certain questions. Dammit, Jack, I thought you'd never ask!"

She twisted her body to embrace him, held him long and hard, her face nestled against the spot where his neck and shoulder joined. Jack felt her tears dampen a spot on his new white shirt; her shoulders quivered. Then she raised her head and kissed him, her lips gentle and warm. At length she pulled away.

"Susan, why are you crying?"

"Because I'm so happy."

"Then why—"

She put a finger against his lips. "You've got a lot to learn about women, Jack Hays. Now, quick, before you change your mind—when?" She moved her finger.

"Yesterday isn't soon enough for me," Jack said, "but there's some unfinished business. When the war's over in Mexico, I'll feel free to resign my Army commission and quit the Rangers. Until then, I'll have to ask you to wait—"

She silenced him with another kiss. "I'll wait, Jack. If it takes two months or ten years, I'll wait."

San Antonio
July 1847

Jack Hays read the last of the reports and letters from the day's mail, leaned back in his chair and stared at the ceiling.

He should have been happier about it all, he thought. The Indians had apparently decided there were healthier hunting grounds than those prowled by Big Pisser and his band of men with big guns and short tempers. He had a good woman waiting and, for a change, a chance to visit her with some regularity.

But the damn war in Mexico kept getting in the way.

The cease-fire hadn't lasted two months. Ben McCulloch had headed south again, grousing that Zachary Taylor couldn't find the outhouse without Ranger help. Ben had done more than help Taylor find the two-holer. He found Santa Anna's main force, rode directly through the Mexican camp at daybreak under the smoky cover of green wood breakfast fires and took his estimate of the enemy troop strength to Taylor. Most of the unofficial reports which reached Jack also credited Ben with helping map out the plan that lured Santa Anna into a trap at Buena Vista, where the Americans severely mauled the Mexican army. Buena Vista should have been the battle that ended the war.

But, Jack thought, things are never as easy as they seem on the surface. The unpleasantness in Mexico was far from over.

Sam Walker had left not long after Ben, but his road back to battle followed a different turn in the trail. Walker's job was to pull General Winfield Scott out of a jam in the drive from Veracruz to Mexico City, the slash that was to end the conflict for good. Scott's campaign had run into serious problems. Guerrilla bands roving the hills harassed the American supply trains, captured Scott's couriers, ambushed his patrols, cut his communication lines. Sam, with two companies of seasoned Rangers in his command, had smashed a half-dozen guerrilla bands. When his Rangers rode back into camp after a foray afield, it was usually with captured horses, saddles, weapons and supplies. But never with prisoners.

Mexicans—civilian and military alike—now lived in mortal fear and dread of the *Rinche* in general, and of Sam Walker in particular. Sam kept the vow he had made as a captive in Perote Prison. He led the drive against Perote and when the fighting ended, he strode to the flagpole in the plaza and dug up the dime he had planted during the Texans' long ordeal at the hated prison.

The legends of Sam Walker and Ben McCulloch grew with each day, and with it the fame of the Texas Rangers and the Colt revolvers they used with such deadly efficiency. The legend spread beyond Texas borders into the columns of eastern newspapers which carried glowing accounts of Ranger exploits. Jack discounted out of hand most of the flowery newspaper reports. He relied more on his own information network and official reports that arrived almost daily at his San Antonio office. By either measurement, Sam Walker and Ben McCulloch stood tall in Texas eyes. That was no surprise to Jack. They had always stood tall to those who had ridden with them. Both held commissions as lieutenant colonels in the American Army, but they were known in the press simply as "the Texas Ranger," or just "Ranger."

Now, "Captain Jack" Hays was about to join them. The message from General Scott had just arrived by courier. Scott was asking Jack to again raise his Ranger regiment, to reinforce General Jo Lane and Walker's men in the faltering campaign against Santa Anna. "Your recommendation to this challenging task comes from President Polk himself," the dispatch concluded. More important to Jack was the brief note from Sam Walker. It read:

Jack:
    Could use some help.
SAM

When a friend asked, a man responded.

FIFTEEN

Veracruz, Mexico
September 1847

Jack Hays had never been so glad to see solid ground in his life as when he stepped from the landing craft onto the beach.

He was sure most of the thousand men in the Ranger regiment filing ashore behind him were equally relieved. The passage to Veracruz had been a stormy one, the ships rolling and bucking in the heavy seas. Jack had spent his share of time at the ship's rail. The queasiness began to pass as he regained his land legs.

"Rough trip, Cap'n."

Jack turned to the muscular, compact man at his side. Ranger Lieutenant John Salmon Ford, Jack's new regimental adjutant, was a bit pale of face himself. Ford had several claims to fame; in addition to being a physician, lawyer, writer and experienced soldier, he was a crack shot with either pistol or rifle. He also possessed a command of profanity that raised cursing to an art form.

"Let's just say I have a newfound respect for sailors," Jack said with a weak smile.

Ford nodded. "No sicker sick than seasick. Got queasy myself a time or two. Was kind of funny, though, watching old Bigfoot draped over a rail heaving his balls up. Ah, what the hell; we'll get over it. General Lane'll be waiting to parley with you, Cap'n. I'll take care of the offloading.''

General Joseph Lane opened the door of his command post himself. "You must be Colonel Jack Hays," Lane said, extending a hand. "Come in, please. You'll never know how glad I am to see you and your men." Lane waved toward a rawhide camp stool. "Have a seat."

Jack sensed that General Jo Lane wasn't one to waste time, so he skipped the formalities and small talk. "What's the situation here, General? I haven't gotten many reports since we left San Antonio."

"Good and bad," Lane said. "General Scott has moved into Mexico City. That's the good news. The bad news is that Santa Anna's pulled his troops out of the capital, and we think he's going to send them against our people along the Veracruz-Mexico City Road."

Lane slid a map from his desk and traced the road from Veracruz through Cerro Gordo, Jalapa, Perote and on to Puebla. "Here's the most pressing problem—Puebla. We've got twenty-two hundred men there under Colonel Childs. The Puebla garrison is under siege from bandits and guerrillas. Childs is holding, but barely. Puebla is the key post in our supply and communication link with Taylor in Mexico City. We've got to hold. And our spies say Santa Anna's on his way there with about five thousand troops."

Lane paused, studying the map. "We have two main objectives here, Colonel Hays. The first is to break the siege at Puebla. The second is to clear the bandits and guerrillas from the entire length of the road from here to Mexico City."

Jack nodded. "We'll get it done, General."

"I never doubted that, Colonel Hays. Your Rangers are to accompany my brigade of regulars to Perote, where we join forces with Colonel Walker's group. How soon can you move out?"

Jack did some quick mental calculations. "By dawn tomorrow, we can be on the road to Perote."

John Ford intercepted Jack on his way back to the men. "Got some good news for a change, Jack," Ford said. "The new Colt pistols are here. Lighter just brought 'em in from an offshore supply ship. A thousand of them. Sam Walker's name's on the manifest."

Jack's interest quickened. "The guns any good?"

"Best I've ever seen," Ford said. "Some improvements over the Walker model. Colt calls 'em the Army Model. Don't know how come. Army's not interested in revolvers. How you want 'em distributed?"

"One for every Ranger who wants it, two if possible. A lot of us are going to keep our old Walker models, I expect. Man doesn't quit a good horse, a good woman or a good gun."

"Can't fault that reasoning, Cap'n Jack. I'll take care of it."

Perote, Mexico
October 1847

Jack Hays held Sam Walker's grip for several seconds, then said, "Oh, the hell with it," and grabbed Walker in a brief bear hug of greeting. When the two separated, unembarrassed at the outward display of emotion, Jack stared into Sam's face for a moment. "Sam, you look tired."

"Been busy out here, Jack. Seems like every damn rancher in the country has a band of guerrillas somewhere on his spread." Sam watched the line of Texas Rangers riding past. Most of them waved or touched a hat brim in salute. Lane's brigade of foot soldiers trailed behind the mounted Rangers. "But now we've got enough men to clear out the *bandidos* and chase old Santa Anna clear to the gates of hell where he belongs. Now, tell me how things are back home," Sam said, a distant look in his blue eyes. "God, how I do miss Texas."

The two men walked toward Sam's headquarters camp, leading their horses. Jack brought Sam up to date on the Indian situation and other news from home. "By the way," he said almost as an afterthought, "I'm going to be a married man soon."

Sam Walker grinned at Jack. "About time some of us Rangers quit playing with guns and grew up. Who's the poor unfortunate girl?"

"Susan Calvert."

"Might have guessed. You always did have an eye for the best fillies in the herd. When?"

"Whenever we get this business finished, Sam."

Sam's grin faded. "Jack, watch your *cojones* out here. These Mexicans are mean, and getting meaner. And Santa Anna's around here somewhere, close. I can all but smell him. I just haven't found him yet."

"We'll find him, Sam."

Thad Green and Bigfoot Wallace cut Santa Anna's trail two days after riding into Perote with Jack. Minutes after the two rode in on lathered horses, Jack, Sam and General Jo Lane crouched around a map Thad sketched in the dust.

"Santa Anna's started toward the El Pinal mountain pass," Thad said. "He's left a garrison and some cannon at Huamantla."

General Lane rubbed a thumb across his chin, his gaze fixed on the dust map. "Gentlemen," he finally said, "we'll have to take Huamantla. That will clear our road into Puebla. We have to get to Colonel Childs soon or we'll lose him. And we need the Huamantla cannon, and any other supplies we can capture, in the Puebla campaign." The general turned to Sam. "Colonel Walker, I'd like you and Colonel Hays to clean out Huamantla. You'll have the dragoons and eight hundred infantry troops from my brigade. Colonel Hays's Rangers will be in the second assault wave. I'll bring the rest of my troops up as reinforcements, should you get caught in a bind. Take Huamantla, gentlemen, and we'll have Puebla safe in hand within a few days."

Huamantla, Mexico
October 1847

Sam Walker reined in his horse a mile from the dusty adobe and masonry town straddling the Veracruz Road. "Jack, this looks like it will be Monterrey all over again. House-to-house work." Sam scanned the horizon. "Any word from the scouts yet?"

"Nothing yet. They're still out."

Sam checked the loads and caps of his Walker Colt and slid it back into the holster. He reached into his pocket and handed a piece of paper to Jack.

"What's this?"

"My new will. If anything happens, see that it's carried out."

"Sam, what the hell—"

Sam Walker waved his troops forward, cutting off Jack's protest. Jack started to spur after Sam but checked the impulse. He waited until Sam's dragoons were a half mile ahead before waving his Rangers into motion.

Jack watched as Sam's command slammed into the first row of defenders. The Americans overran the first line of defense; a few minutes later, they had carried the fight well into the village. From the sounds of battle Jack could tell that Sam was gaining ground rapidly.

"Scout coming hell for leather, Jack," Bigfoot Wallace said at Jack's side.

Jack spurred out to meet the rider. Thad Green pulled his lathered and blowing horse to a stop. "Captain Jack, Santa Anna's doubled back! It looks like the whole damn Mexican Army's moving up to hit Sam!"

"Get to Lane, Thad! Tell him to throw everything he's got in behind us!" Jack whirled his horse, spurred back to the Rangers. The firing in Huamantla grew to a steady, rolling thunder. "Bigfoot, take the right flank! I've got the left!" Jack drew his handgun. "Let's go, men!" he yelled.

Cannon shells whistled into the mass of charging Rangers and burst into a deadly rain of fragments. Rifle and pistol balls churned the air as Jack's men stormed into Huamantla, their horses leaping bodies and barricades in the narrow, dusty streets. Jack pulled his black to a stop, aimed and fired toward a Mexican rifleman on a rooftop. The man's body jerked and slid from sight.

The attack became a whirling melee of bodies, men afoot and on horseback struggling through a thick blanket of dust and powder smoke that obscured vision and choked the breath from man and beast. The two armies clashed head-on near the central plaza. Jack felt the tug of a rifle ball against his shirtsleeve. He ignored the near miss and turned to yell at John Ford a few feet away: "Cannon up ahead! Let's take 'em!"

Jack drove spurs into the black and swept past a cluster of dragoons pinned down by rifle fire from the Mexican battery. He heard the Texan war whoops and clatter of hooves behind him, then the black jumped, cleared the barricade protecting the cannon and came down almost on top of a Mexican gun crew. Jack emptied his pistol at the cannoneers and saw one of them crumple. Then Ford and other Rangers swept over the gun emplacement, firing pistols and shotguns, swinging Bowie knives, sabers and clubbed rifles. The battle swirled across the town square into a cluster of houses beyond. Jack dismounted and slipped his double-barrel shotgun from the roll behind the cantle. He fired one barrel into the doorway of a house, a second toward a window, then shifted the shotgun to his left hand and pulled his second pistol. Under the covering fire John Ford and three other Rangers stormed the house, yelling, shooting and slashing. Seconds later the house was in American hands.

Santa Anna threw his army into a counterattack; the Mexican infantry charge slammed into heavy fire from American weapons and faltered for a moment as the Texans held their ground. Seconds seemed to drag into hours for Jack. The sting of dust, sweat and smoke blurred his vision. Then a mass of blue-clad soldiers poured across the town square and Lane's infantry ripped into the massed Mexican troops.

A half hour later it was over.

Santa Anna's bugler sounded the retreat. American soldiers turned captured guns on the fleeing Mexican army, sending ball and canister into the ranks. Huamantla was in American hands. But the Americans had no opportunity to pursue. The soldiers were too weary, and running short of ammunition and water. A hundred Rangers harassed the retreating Mexicans with rifle fire and mounted skirmishes, taking a heavy toll, until they too were forced to abandon the chase.

Jack leaned against the black horse's shoulder and wiped a hand across his eyes. When he looked up, Thad Green stood before him, tears streaming down his cheeks, his face ash-white.

"What is it, Thad? You hurt again?"

Thad shook his head. "It's Sam, Jack. He's dead."

Jack felt the slam of ice into his gut. *Christ, not Sam; it can't be.* "Where?"

"Northeast edge of the square." Thad slumped against a wall, let his body slide down the rough adobe until he squatted, head between his knees, arms crossed. He still held a pistol in one hand.

Jack found Sam Walker's body surrounded by a crowd of Rangers and Army regulars. There wasn't a dry eye among them. The sandy red curls in the back of Sam's head were soaked in blood. Jack knelt beside the body of his longtime friend, the ache in his chest building, tears stinging the corners of his eyes. He lifted Sam's prized Walker Colt from lifeless fingers. He sat and stared at Sam, the weapon held loose in his palm. The cylinder was still warm to the touch.

"Colonel Hays," a young dragoon lieutenant said, "I'll get a burial detail ready."

"Like hell you will!" Jack barked. "Nobody is burying Sam Walker in Mexican soil!"

Jack felt a hand on his shoulder. "Of course they won't, Colonel Hays," General Jo Lane said. "I'll have a caisson rigged. We'll have a detail take his body home to Texas. He was one of the bravest and best men I've ever known."

That night, Jack sat and stared into the flicker of the small camp fire, unable to eat. He still cradled Sam Walker's Colt, serial number 1020, in a palm, as if by touching it he could still touch Sam.

"You sent for me, Colonel Hays?" Captain Bedney F. McDonald stood before Jack, his dragoon cap in hand.

"Yes, Captain. This afternoon I read Sam Walker's last will, handed to me just before the shooting started at Huamantla. He wanted you to have his Walker Colt." Jack handed the pistol to the captain.

"But, sir, I know how much Sam thought of you, and you of Sam. Perhaps it would be better if you kept it."

"No, Captain. Sam wanted you to have it."

Moisture glinted at the corners of McDonald's eyes. "Thank you, Colonel. Sam asked me once if I would return it to Colonel Colt if—if anything happened to him. I'll see that Colonel Colt gets it." McDonald held the weapon reverently as he strode from Jack's camp.

Thad Green appeared at Jack's fire a few minutes later.

"Jack," Thad said, "General Lane wants to know if you want to help take Sam's body back to Texas. He said he could give you a two-week furlough."

Jack shook his head. "I think I'll stay and finish what Sam set out to do. That's what he would want."

The caisson bearing Sam Walker's casket, draped in the American flag, rolled slowly between the two long rows of men on each side of the road north from Huamantla at dawn the next day.

Behind the caisson walked Sam's favorite horse, saddle empty and the boots reversed in the stirrups. An honor guard of twenty Texas Rangers and thirty United States Army dragoons bracketed the caisson. General Lane's entire brigade had turned out to pay their respects, the men freshly shaved and in clean uniforms. They were the first in line. The Texas Rangers were next, each man baring his head in silent salute as the procession passed. Men hardened to battle and accustomed to death wept openly and without shame as Sam's body passed.

Jack Hays waited alone at the north end of the column, astride his black horse. He removed his hat as the caisson rolled by. He watched until the procession had become small in the distance, then rejoined his men. None of them spoke. Jack read past the pain in their eyes to the cold anger beneath, noted the grim set of jawlines and saw his own feelings mirrored there. *God have mercy on any Mexican soldier, bandit or guerrilla,* he thought, *because this bunch of Texas Rangers sure as hell won't.*

Tlaxcala, Mexico
November 1847

Jack Hays reloaded his Walker Colt and gazed across the guerrilla camp dotted with the bodies of more than forty of Jiminez Perez's irregulars. It had been more of a massacre than a fight. Fifty Rangers had ridden three straight days and through two nights to hit Perez at dawn. *This one was worth it,* Jack thought; *the word will spread that not even Jiminez Perez's band was safe from the Texas Rangers.*

The Perez bandits were the last of the major guerrilla bands who plied their deadly trade along the Veracruz to Mexico City road. Being a *robador* was fast losing its appeal among the Mexican partisans. The chance of running afoul of the Texas Devils took a lot of the shine from the glory of fighting for the mother country. It was one thing to be a successful bandit smashing small *gringo* patrols and lone couriers. It was quite another to be shot dead in your sleep by a large band of madmen.

"Captain Jack, there's six of them still alive," Thad Green said.

"Tie them up. A nice long walk back to Puebla should be good for their souls. Any sign of old Perez?"

"No, Captain," Thad said. "Some of the men are still looking—" The sound was like the slap of a hand against a slab of beef; Thad's head snapped back. The shock of a heavy slug hammered the slender frame to the ground.

Jack stared for a second, stunned, at the crumpled form. The left side of Thad's head was gone. Jack heard 'Gator Davis's scream of rage and pain, saw the burly Ranger sprint toward the corrals behind the ranch house, Bigfoot Wallace close behind. John Ford knelt at Thad's side, took one look at the body, then rose and put a hand on Jack's shoulder. "Thad never knew what hit him, Cap'n. At least he didn't suffer."

Jack swallowed hard against the wave of pain and grief that clamped against his throat. Then he lifted his pistol and strode toward the corral. Bigfoot and Davis met Jack twenty paces from the corral. 'Gator's Bowie knife rested against the edge of a Mexican's throat. Blood seeped from beneath the blade.

"Caught the bastard trying to climb on a horse," Davis said. "Barrel of his rifle's still hot. Let me carve on him a while, Jack. Dammit, Thad was my friend."

Jack stared into the eyes of Jiminez Perez for several seconds. The bandit leader's swarthy face was twisted in raw terror. "Take the knife away, 'Gator."

"Dammit, Jack! You can't let him live after this!"

"Do as I say!"

Davis grudgingly lowered the knife. Hope flared in Perez's eyes, and the beginnings of a smirk touched the corners of the thin lips. Perez pulled himself erect. "I am your prisoner," he said.

Jack raised his pistol and shot Perez between the eyes.

"Thad was my friend too, 'Gator." Jack heard the cold hardness in his own voice. "Cut Perez's head off and stick it on a stake by the road. Let it be a warning to any Mexican bandit who kills a Ranger. Then wreck this place. Burn whatever will burn. Leave a Ranger calling card." Jack spun on a heel and stalked away.

John Ford fell into step as Jack strode toward the waiting horses. "Cap'n Jack, I didn't know Thad as well as the rest of you, but I liked the kid. It's my job to notify the family, but you want to write a note, too?"

Jack swallowed against the pain in his gut. "Yes, I do. And we won't bury him here, either. Get his body ready to go back to Texas, John. Thad Green was a hell of a good Ranger. He earned his right to be buried in Texas soil."

Puebla, Mexico
November 1847

Jack Hays stood in General Jo Lane's office in the bullet-pocked central plaza where only a few weeks before Lane's brigade, led by Jack's Rangers, had swept the Mexican forces from the siege of Colonel Childs's command.

Jack wondered idly why he had been summoned. The road was now clear of Mexican bandits, hunted down and eliminated by wide-ranging Ranger patrols under Jack, Alligator Davis, John Ford and Bigfoot Wallace. Reinforcements and supplies now flowed freely along the Veracruz road to Mexico City, where General Winfield Scott was in firm control.

Jo Lane stood beside the fireplace, an elbow draped over a corner of the mantel. "Colonel Hays, I've been asked to express President Polk's personal appreciation for the service you and your Rangers have rendered here. I must admit I'm a little awed at the speed and efficiency with which you cleared the Veracruz road of guerrillas."

Jack shrugged. "My men did that, sir. The Mexican bandits met more than their match in Texans who cut their war teeth on Comanche campaigns. We took what we learned from the Indian wars and turned it against the Mexicans. I can't take credit for that."

"Nonetheless, you were the commander who put the campaign together. Your guerrilla-fighting tactics may well show up in a military training manual one day." Lane pushed away from the fireplace, dug a slim cigar from a tunic pocket. "That's not the only reason I asked you to come." Lane crouched, probed the fireplace with a pair of tongs, retrieved a live coal and fired his cigar. "We're going to Mexico City, Colonel Hays. Our assignment—yours, primarily—will be to clean out the last of the irregulars and guerrillas in that region. And to try to capture General Santa Anna."

Jack breathed a slow sigh. *So the end is that close,* he thought. *Mexico must be very near to surrender.* "Yes, sir. We'll be ready to move when you give the word. I have patrols in the field, but we're in touch with them regularly. I can call them in, most any time."

"Very good, Colonel Hays." Lane puffed at the cigar and wrinkled his nose in distaste. "Mexican tobacco. Like smoking hemp. Lord, what I wouldn't give for a good Virginia burley." Lane squinted through the blue-gray haze. "Jack, I've been curious about something. You're a full colonel, but your men call you 'Captain Jack.' May I ask why they don't refer to you by your proper rank?"

Jack smiled. "Sir, rank doesn't mean squat to a Texas Ranger. To them, 'Captain' is a title of respect. It's the highest title that exists in a Ranger's mind. It's a hell of an honor, sir, and I hope I never lose it."

Jo Lane nodded. "I understand now. And I doubt seriously you'll ever lose it." Lane leaned over the desk and slid open a drawer. "There's one more thing. I saved the Texas flag that Sam Walker raised over Perote Prison." He held out the folded, wind-frayed banner. "I thought you might like to raise it over Mexico City, Captain Jack."

SIXTEEN

Mexico City
January 1848

Jack Hays returned General Winfield Scott's steady glare. Old Fuss and Feathers, as the Rangers had tabbed Scott, was not a happy man.

"You sent for me, General?"

Scott sputtered for a moment, trying with little success to contain his anger. "Colonel Hays, I want to know what you intend to do about this massacre of civilians by your Rangers."

Jack lifted an eyebrow. "Massacre, General?"

Scott rapped his knuckles against the top of the desk. "Don't be coy with me, Colonel Hays! You know full well what I mean! A Mexican steals a simple neckerchief and is shot dead in the street. Another throws a stone at a Ranger and dies from a pistol ball. And now this!" Scott waved toward the street outside. "Eighty Mexicans lying dead in the morgue across the way! And for what reason?"

Jack shrugged. "A Ranger was murdered last evening. Fellow by the name of Adam Allsens. I suppose the men just followed the biblical adage of an eye for an eye."

"Dammit, man, you're their commanding officer! Put a stop to this outrage! Immediately!"

"That might be difficult, General Scott," Jack said. "When a Ranger is struck, he doesn't turn the other cheek. He hits back.

As hard as he can. You may not approve of his methods, but you certainly won't misunderstand his message." Jack drew a deep breath. He was beginning to get a bit irritated himself. "General Scott, no man imposes on a Texas Ranger without the sure and certain knowledge that he will pay for his act. When we first rode into Mexico City, the locals were murdering several Americans a week. I do believe that practice will stop now."

Scott abruptly sighed and plopped into a chair. "Very well, Colonel Hays. I've been told how futile it is to try to instill discipline in a Texas Ranger. I'll just have to find work for your men outside Mexico City."

"That would please us no end, General Scott," Jack said. "If there's nothing else?"

Scott dismissed Jack with a wave of disgust.

Jack stepped into the street and elbowed his way through the throng of humanity to the Ranger quarters. John Ford, now universally known as "Rip," was waiting at the door. As regimental adjutant, one of Ford's duties was to notify the next of kin of a Ranger's death. Wanting to add a more personal touch, he had written "Rest In Peace" at the end of each letter; but as casualties mounted and Ford found himself pressed for time, he started abbreviating the personal message to "R.I.P." One of the Rangers offhandedly referred to him as "Old Rip," and the nickname stuck.

"Got a line on that egg-suckin' sonofabitch Santa Anna, Jack," Rip said. "Bigfoot and 'Gator Davis cut sign on him outside Tehuacan. Got about a hundred cavalry with him."

The excitement of the hunt shoved aside the last traces of Jack's anger at General Scott. "Get Company C horseback, Rip. I'll tell Jo Lane what we're up to."

Tehuacan, Mexico
January 1848

Rip Ford stood in the doorway of the empty living quarters and let fly a string of curses that would bring envy to a muleskinner. Jack Hays listened in admiration to Ford's eloquence with the earthier words in the English language. "Dammit all to hell," Rip wound down his grousing, "we march all day and all night and still come up a day late and a dollar short. That potbellied butcher got away again."

Jack stepped past Rip into the quarters. A cloth was laid on a long table in the large room, candles still burning. A crystal ink-stand had overturned on a white satin mat across a writing desk. Jack touched a fingertip to the ink. It was still sticky.

"Somebody left in a big hurry, Rip. We couldn't have missed them by much."

"Yeah. Dammit, if we hadn't been slowed down by those foot soldiers we'd have had the sonofabitch."

"General Lane had his orders," Jack said. "If you're going to blame somebody, blame General Scott. Old Fuss and Feathers must have been afraid we might wrinkle Santa Anna's uniform or something."

Jack heard his name called from the far end of the room where a stack of trunks and a burnished brass bedstead stood. Several Rangers and infantrymen from Lane's regiment were prowling through the trunks.

The hoard yielded a small slipper and dozens of dresses owned by Doña Santa Anna. One of the more striking articles of clothing in the trunks was a fifteen-pound coat embossed and embroidered in solid gold, obviously Santa Anna's formal dress tunic.

'Gator Davis yelped in excitement. From the bottom of one trunk he drew a long, tapered case covered in green velvet. Inside was a cane with a polished iron staff, its head sporting an ornately carved eagle of gold. The eagle held a massive diamond in its beak; rubies, sapphires, emeralds and more diamonds studded the eagle and the pedestal upon which it rested. "My God, have you ever seen such a thing," Davis said, twisting the cane in his hands.

"Give it to Captain Jack!" one of the Rangers called. The entire company took up the cry. Davis thrust the elaborate cane into Jack's hands. Jack turned it in his fingers, admiring the sheer beauty of the workmanship.

"It'll make one hell of a trophy, Captain Jack. Something to remember old Santa Anna by," Davis said.

"Gentlemen, I thank you," Jack said. "I'll keep it for the time being. But the only real trophy I want is Santa Anna. He got away this time, but he can't run forever."

An hour later, General Jo Lane sat at the table so recently abandoned by Antonio Lopez de Santa Anna and distributed the spoils of the raid. The Mexican general's gold-laden dress coat went to the State of Texas. Other articles of Santa Anna's clothing, personal items and pieces of furniture were distributed among the men. "Doña Santa Anna's things will be returned to the trunks and delivered to her when possible," Lane said. "The American Army of Occupation does not make war against women."

None of the Rangers objected. They had no personal quarrel with the woman. It was her husband they wanted.

The festivities triggered by the discovery of Santa Anna's possessions faded as the Rangers and Lane's infantry turned back toward Mexico City. Jack felt the mood shift among his men, and he knew why. Santa Anna was still at large.

The patrol had been back in the capital city only a few hours before Major William H. Polk walked into Jack's small headquarters office on a narrow side street off the central plaza. Jack had known Major Polk only a few weeks, but instinctively liked the tall, broad-shouldered brother of the President of the United States. "Major Polk," Jack said, extending a hand. "Something I can do for you?"

Polk hesitated, obviously embarrassed. "Colonel Hays, I hate to ask, and if you decline my request, I'll certainly understand. I've come about Santa Anna's cane."

Jack hefted the green velvet case from its casual perch in a corner. "A garish bit of excess on Santa Anna's part when his men are barefoot, short of ammunition and hungry," he said. He slipped the cane from its case and laid it across his cluttered desk.

"Colonel, I know that cane was a gift to you from your men. An expression of appreciation and fondness. But I wondered—" the major stammered slightly "—if you would consider giving it up. I know it's worth a great deal to you, both financially and as a memento. But it would mean so much to my brother, as a symbol of this nasty little war."

Jack slipped the cane back into its case and handed it to the officer. "Major Polk, this cane means little to me, aside from the fact that it was presented to me by my men, and they've given me a damn sight more than that over the years. If you think President Polk would like it, then by all means he may have it."

"Colonel Hays, I—"

"I do have one request, Major," Jack interrupted. "Please inform the president that Santa Anna's cane is a gift from the Texas Rangers."

The worried expression faded from Polk's face. "Colonel Hays, you may rest assured that he will be so informed. I thank you for your consideration. I know of no way to repay your generosity."

"No repayment needed," Jack said. "Let's just win this war and go home. All I need is waiting for me there."

Jalapa, Mexico
January 1848

Jack Hays unsaddled the black, scooped a double handful of grain into the *morral* and slipped the feed bag over Justin's head. The five-day patrol through guerrilla country had brought but one quick skirmish, and that ended when the Mexican bandits threw down their weapons and fled into the brush after the first Ranger charge.

Resistance even in bandit country was fading rapidly, Jack reflected. His Rangers had killed less than ten guerrillas in two weeks of combing the rugged hills around Mexico City. The patrols, Jack knew, were mostly make-work designed to keep his men out of the city and away from the civilian populace. General Scott still bore a grudge from the Ranger's reign of vengeance in Mexico City. But the number of American deaths at Mexican hands had dropped sharply there since that day. The locals never knew when the *Rinche* might ride back into town, and the killing of Americans wasn't worth the risk.

Jack spread his saddle blanket to dry and listened to the rumble in his gut, a not so gentle reminder he hadn't eaten in almost twenty hours. Neither had most of the hundred other Rangers who had filtered back to the camp, their scattered twenty-to-forty-man patrols complete.

Jack was laying wood for a fire when Alligator Davis rode into camp at a fast trot. "General Lane's on his way here," Davis said. "He asked me to tell you to gather the Rangers, call in any patrols still out and stick tight until he gets here. Santa Anna's quit the fight, Captain Jack. The war's all but over. We'll be going home soon."

The cloak of saddle weariness fell from Jack's shoulders. He stood silent for a moment, staring into 'Gator Davis's face, and felt a smile spread through the dust that frosted his own beard. Then he shook himself back to reality. Jack Hays knew he wasn't going to feel at home until Justin's hooves hit Texas dirt. He gestured toward the fire. "Hungry, 'Gator?"

"I'd eat this horse if I didn't hate to walk."

General Jo Lane rode into the Ranger camp at sundown, the dragoons in his wake. Lane touched the brim of his campaign hat in greeting, then dismounted and tossed the reins to a sergeant. "Captain Jack, a word with you in private, please."

Jack led General Lane to the edge of the camp, where a clump of scrub cedar provided a measure of privacy. "Jack, we've got a problem," Lane said. "Santa Anna's going to be coming down the road by this camp tomorrow. Right into the teeth of your Rangers. He's been given a safe conduct pass as part of the peace negotiations. I know how these men of yours feel about the general. I share their feelings. But we *must* let him pass safely or risk prolonging the war. Can you control your men, stop them from killing Santa Anna?"

Jack smiled. "Believe it or not, General Lane, it *is* possible to control Texas Rangers. You just have to know when it's important to do so, and how to go about it."

Word of Santa Anna's approach spread like a wind-blown prairie fire through the Ranger ranks. Jack Hays stood silent and listened to the furious mutters from the assembled hundred or so

Rangers, letting them take the edge from their rage with words. Then he called for quiet. The grumbling subsided.

"Gentlemen," Jack said, "we've ridden through a lot together. We've all lost friends at Mexican hands. Now, you've heard General Lane say that the penalty for violation of a safe conduct pass is death. I know that doesn't mean spit to most of you. I doubt there's a man here who would not gladly trade his own life for the pleasure of slitting Santa Anna's throat."

A low mutter of agreement swept through the ranks. Jack waited for it to pass. "I would remind you of one thing." Jack raised his voice for emphasis. "Santa Anna *is* traveling under a safe conduct pass granted by our commanding general. To take his life under such conditions would be murder. More importantly, *you would dishonor the name of the State of Texas!*"

The silence in the group stretched into several heartbeats. Finally, Bigfoot Wallace shrugged. "Then, by God, we won't do it," he said. "We'll let him pass."

First one, then another Ranger nodded in agreement. "He don't deserve to live, Cap'n Jack," one man called out, "but we'll go along with you. That doesn't have to stop us from scaring the piss out of him—and we don't have to do a solitary thing but sit and watch him go by."

Jack turned to General Jo Lane. "Santa Anna won't be harmed, General," he said. "The Texas Rangers have given their word."

Jack Hays calmed the nervous black with a gentle pat on the neck and glanced along the Jalapa Road. A single carriage with a brightly uniformed Mexican cavalry escort approached in the distance.

Jack turned, his gaze sweeping the double line of Rangers, more than fifty on each side of the narrow road, all mounted, heavily armed, their bearded faces grim. A stony silence held as the carriage approached; not a man spoke. Santa Anna's open carriage entered the gauntlet. Jack watched the rotund Mexican pass, his eyes fixed straight ahead, his face noticeably pale. *I don't blame you for being scared, General,* Jack thought, *and I hope you carry that feeling to your grave.* He forced himself to give Santa Anna credit for one thing—if the man truly believed he faced death here, he sat erect and outwardly calm, prepared to meet his end with the dignity of a soldier.

At Santa Anna's side sat his wife, a pretty, petite woman. A gentle smile touched the corners of her mouth; from time to time she offered a small nod of greeting toward the double line of horsemen. Santa Anna's daughter rode in the rear seat. Her expression mirrored that of her father. If she felt fear, it was concealed by a quiet inner courage.

The cavalrymen escorting the general glanced nervously from one side to the other. It was probably, Jack thought, their first face-to-face encounter with the dreaded Texas Devils. He expected it would make a lasting impression.

The coach moved at a steady pace down the double line of Texans, emerged at the far end. There had been not a single taunt or threatening move from the Rangers, only the hard glare of some two hundred eyes. Santa Anna's cortege passed from view. The Rangers broke ranks and returned to camp.

Mexico City
March 1848

Jack Hays sat astride the black in the center of the front rank of assembled Texas Rangers. The anticipation was almost a tangible thing. Men spoke in muted voices. The horses also sensed the excitement, stamping hooves and tossing their heads, jangling bits and curb chains.

General Winfield Scott strode toward the low wooden stand which had been erected for the final review of the Texas volunteers. The war with Mexico was over; the Treaty of Guadalupe Hidalgo had grown from rumor to fact. In one stroke of the pen the United States of America had gained a vast territory stretching from the Gulf Coast and the Rio Grande south and west through California, and north beyond Santa Fe into the Rocky Mountain range. It was the largest single land acquisition in the nation's history.

Most important to Jack Hays, and the men who rode with him, was that Texas had survived. That made it worth the sacrifices.

The war might be over, Jack thought, but the problems with Mexico would not end overnight. Mutual hate and distrust ran too deep. *At least my part in it is over; soon Jack Hays will be a Ranger no more, but a happily married civilian surveyor.* He touched Susan's last letter resting in his breast pocket, as if by doing so he could reach across the miles to stroke the hand that penned it. Susan wrote that she had started planning the wedding before the ink was dry on the treaty that ended the war, "and don't think for a minute you're going to get out of it, Jack Hays." She added. "My parents are already starting to hint at grandchildren, so come home quickly, before they become totally insufferable."

General Winfield Scott mounted the reviewing stand and stood silent for a moment, looking across the gathering of more than seven hundred survivors of Jack Hays's Texas regiment. In a place of honor behind the front ranks a single horse stood, saddle empty, in memory of those who had fallen in battle. Scott raised his hand to his hat in a crisp military salute.

"Gentlemen of Texas, the Army of Occupation of Mexico is no more," Scott said. His crisp, clear voice carried to the far ranks of Rangers. "I wish to express the appreciation of the government of the United States of America for your valued service. And now, it is my duty and my privilege to dismiss you from that service, and to wish you a safe return to your home state."

A thunderous cheer erupted from Ranger throats.

The tumult set Jack's horse to fidgeting. He stroked Justin's neck to calm him and waited until the shouts began to fade. Then he kneed his horse forward and whirled the black to face the men he had served with for so long.

The cheers merged into one chant from the Ranger ranks: "Captain Jack, Captain Jack, Captain Jack—" Jack raised a hand for quiet and swallowed against the knot in his throat. *My God, these are good men,* he thought. *What the hell can I possibly say to let them know how I feel about them?*

He decided to say the one thing they most wanted to hear.

"Gentlemen," Captain Jack Hays called, "Texas waits! Let's go home!"

EPILOGUE

John Coffee (Jack) Hays resigned his commission in the Texas Rangers upon his return to the state at the end of the war with Mexico, and married Susan Calvert. In 1849 he led a caravan to California, where he served as sheriff of San Francisco County. Appointed surveyor general of California, he laid out the city of Oakland. He amassed a substantial fortune and became prominent in national politics. While he made his home in California, he made frequent visits to Texas. He died near Piedmont, California, on April 25, 1883. Hays County, Texas, is named in his honor.

W. A. A. (Bigfoot) Wallace remained active in the Texas Rangers, serving as a captain during the border wars and in Indian campaigns, operated a small ranch and worked as a stage driver. He never married. He died January 7, 1899, and is buried in the State Cemetery in Austin, Texas.

Ben McCulloch also went to California in 1849, serving as sheriff of Sacramento County and later as a United States Marshal. In May 1861 he was commissioned a brigadier general in the Confederate Army, and on March 7, 1862, at the Battle of Elk Horn, he was killed by Union sharpshooters. He was still carrying his Walker Colt at the time of his death. He was buried with full military honors in the State Cemetery in Austin, Texas.

John Salmon (Rip) Ford became an editor and publisher, a frontier explorer, a Texas senator and a Texas Ranger captain serving in the Rio Grande during the border war against Juan Cortina. He was a leader in two major Indian battles in the Texas

Panhandle. With the outbreak of the Civil War he was commissioned a colonel in the 2nd Texas Cavalry, with a command in the Rio Grande district. He was a charter member of the Texas State Historical Association. He died in San Antonio, Texas, November 3, 1897.

General Zachary Taylor, propelled into the national spotlight by his success in the war with Mexico, became the twelfth President of the United States of America.

About the Author

Gene Shelton is a lifelong Texas resident, raised on a ranch in the Panhandle. As a youth, he worked as a ranch hand and horse trainer, and rode the amateur rodeo circuit as a bull rider and calf roper.

He is the author of *Last Gun*, Book One in the Texas Legends series, as well as two other acclaimed Western novels, *Track of the Snake* and *Day of the Scorpion*. He has been an active member of the Western Writers of America, Inc., since 1981.

A newspaperman by trade, he has been a reporter for the *Amarillo Globe-News* and the *Dallas Times Herald*. His most recent assignments were as managing editor of the *Sulphur Springs News-Telegram* and as copy editor for the *Tyler Courier-Times*. He has also written numerous magazine articles for *The Quarter Horse Journal*, *The Ranchman,* and *Black Belt Magazine*.

He has taught fiction-writing classes at several colleges and universities in the East Texas area.

APR   1992